TINSEL AND TEMPTATION: A HOLIDAY ANTHOLOGY

Paperback ISBN: 978-0-9906942-8-1

Cover design by Teresa Spreckelmeyer of Be My Bard

TABLE OF CONTENTS

ONCE UPON A KIDNAPPED SANTA

DELILAH DAWSON

Finally, the perfect holiday! Virginia Parker sighed. Surely, most of her friends thought she was nuts for celebrating by herself at the family cabin, but it was better than the alternative. There were always friends who invited her over to their home, but she couldn't help but feel that her invitations were offered out of love …along with a dose of worry and pity. Worry, she could understand. The pity had started to define the holidays, so she'd decided on doing something different.

This cabin was the perfect place for a solo location. Solo-cation! Yes, a new word to describe vacationing alone. She eyed the half-filled wineglass wondering what other words would be revealed by the time the wine was gone.

She swirled the liquid and addressed an imaginary friend. "Me? I was solo-cating at the cabin. It was snowing and I was warm and cozy… absolutely fabulous!"

Not that it was a lie. The winter cabin was cozy, Christmas carols filled the air, and the aroma of roast in the oven was divine. Looking around and feeling slightly tipsy, she admired the rustic holiday décor and spent a nostalgic moment remembering how her mother had once used them in holidays past. There were decorations from the Kwanza phase of her childhood (her mother had only celebrated a few years) mixed in with some Jewish ornaments (from a neighbor that had been her mother's best friend) and outdated, fragile ornaments that were falling apart at the seams. But she just didn't have the heart to throw a single one out.

There was also a childhood family portrait, her parents and brother sporting fashionable afros while she had her hair woven into cute circular cornrows. Those were the days when the holiday seasons had been so full and perfect.

With her wineglass in hand, she was heading toward the couch facing the fireplace when the cabin door unexpectedly flew open, a flurry of snowflakes chasing two burly bodies that crashed to the ground, feet away from where she stood. There was grunt and a string of profanities when one man head-butted the other, appearing to break his nose.

It took one blink for two things to become immediately clear.

One of the men was her brother, wearing what was once a nice tuxedo, but was now splattered in red from a bloody nose.

The other man wore a Santa suit, was bound and gagged, and was fighting like a mercenary instead of a jolly old Santa.

Moving quickly, Virginia reached into the pantry for the shotgun and racked one in the chamber. Even over the angelic Christmas carols, the sound of the loaded shotgun was unmistakable.

Both men froze.

She aimed between them. "Goddamnit, Brian. It's Christmas Frickin' Eve. I swear, I —"

"Sis, I'm sorry!" He stared with his bloodied mouth hanging open.

She glowered and nudged the air with the shotgun to encourage him to explain further.

"I know it looks bad, but I didn't know what to do!" Brian continued. "It wasn't supposed to be him!"

The Santa made a sound like a growling Rottweiler, the gag he wore barely muffling the sound. Brian crawled away then stood, his whole body practically twitching.

"I was just doing a … a romantic thing. I was going to," Brian's fingers made invisible, twitchy quote marks in the air, "kidnap Tommy for the weekend,—"

"Kidnap?!"

"Tommy was doing this Santa gig at the hospital and I had this plan to grab him when he was done, take him home and—"

"Oh-dear-God." The lovely wine buzz she'd had suddenly throbbed at her temples. She lowered the shotgun just enough, avoiding the temptation to actually shoot her brother while she had the chance. Santa had managed to kneel, then rock backward onto his heels to stand despite his hands being tied behind his back. His eyes were starting to look slightly familiar, bringing a sudden queasiness to the pit of her stomach. Nope, definitely not a helpless old Santa.

She removed her finger from the trigger but kept the shotgun at hip level. "You kidnapped a hospital Santa?"

"I know how this looks, but it was for a romantic getaway."

"It's called a crime, you idiot!"

"No! Wait just a sec. You know Tommy and I have been dating and ... and it's our three month anniversary, so, you know, he really digs role-playing, and I just knew he'd get a kick out of me kidnapping him... "—his fingers quickly came up to emphasize the quotes again—"and... and..." By now, Brian's voice quivered, had began to spiral to a weepy, high-pitched falsetto.

"Geez, Bri, you frickin' kidnapped a stranger?!"

"Well, ummm." Brian, his eyes big as saucers, looked truly distraught. He wiped at his bloodied nose and pleaded with his wide palms. "I... He... It's all a big mistake!"

"For the love of–!" She clenched her teeth to keep from spewing the vitriol boiling in her brain. "Why didn't you let him go?"

"He wouldn't stop fighting! I was driving the van, and Bubba decided to tie him up—"

"Bubba's involved with this?" She cringed at the thought of her beefy cousin being involved in any way. Whenever Bubba did a favor, you sure as hell owed him one.

"Yeah," Brian confirmed without the slightest remorse.

"Where's Bubba now?"

"He asked me to drop him off at his momma's."

Of course, sure. "Un-be-frickin-lievable," she mumbled.

A second growl had Virginia adjusting her shotgun. Even without taking the fake Santa beard off, the familiarity of the gagged stranger was stirring up a memory.

Almost immediately, her brother took a big step toward the door, where more snow was swirling in, robbing her small cabin of heat. "I panicked. I didn't know where else to go!"

"You could've just cut Santa loose and apologized."

"When we tried that, but he almost knocked Bubba's teeth out!"

"Imagine that."

"Look, I'm so sorry, honest to God. But ... shit, my nose hurts like hell. Can I at least get a paper towel?"

Virginia gritted her teeth some more, eying the way the blood oozing from his nose was covering his chin like a red goatee. His left eye looked slightly swollen, but his black skin probably would hide the bruise for a while. Reluctantly, she stepped around the island to reach the paper towels when, from the corner of her eye, she saw Brian bolt.

"Brian, don't you dare!"

Brian sprinted out the door and into the storm. Virginia chased after him, but he was already circling toward his van in the swirling snow, shouting a stream of high-pitched apologies as he made his getaway, finishing loudly with, "I GOTTA GO FIND TOMMY!"

She aimed the shotgun at the red taillights, but the van lurched forward, swerving in the snow. Fear for his safety had her heart pounding, and she reluctantly lowered the weapon.

Growling helplessly at the disappearing vehicle, she stood and mentally screeched, visceral disappointment settling in her soul. Well, if he thought she was going to clean up his mess once more, he was sadly mistaken.

Pivoting, she marched back indoors through the calf-high snow, her fuzzy slippers completely wet and cold, her holiday cheer completely ruined.

The pissed-off Santa stood in the open space of the living-room/kitchen area, using the counter corner to try to scrape the rope from his wrists. The Santa hat was sewn to the fake beard and both were askew, and his fake belly listed to the side, but he didn't look any less dangerous. Those familiar eyes followed her every move, and already she dreaded the sinking feeling in her gut that told her he was no stranger. With a sigh, she grabbed the remote from the counter and lowered the volume on the music.

"Look," she said, speaking gently and flashing a friendly smile, "I'm really sorry for what my stupid brother put you through." Walking forward carefully, she continued to speak calmly. "Let me remove the gag and the, um, ropes, and we can talk."

He growled, and she wasn't sure if he was acknowledging her request or threatening her if she stepped closer. She paused, narrowed her gaze at him and decided they could both benefit from her taking a sip of wine, so she took a healthy, unladylike gulp of Chardonnay.

He turned his back, offered his bound wrists, then glanced at her over his shoulder, his gaze positively icy. And that's when the recognition hit. Carefully, she placed the wineglass on the counter and removed his Santa hat and beard to be sure.

Oh effing hell! It was Dominic Coscano! The guy who could've been her high-school sweetheart, if only life hadn't intervened.

Dominic was the golden child of an Italian-Mexican clan of about a hundred cousins of dangerous and questionable reputations, crazies that would ride their thundering, battle-scarred vehicles into hell to rescue.

He'd been in her youthful daydreams and more than one adult wet dream. It was infuriating that even now, he had this heart-palpitating effect on her.

Oh, Dear Lord, it was Dom! Part of her was giddy with awe and disbelief. Another part of her wanted to ship him immediately back to town, or the North Pole.

Exhaling carefully, she looked him over once more. This was not a problem. She could handle it. They were both intelligent and level-headed adults. And he was the kind of guy to play Santa for some kids in a hospital on Christmas Eve, not murder a woman in a cabin. Except that right at this moment, he didn't look so different from his hellion brothers.

While trying to undo the gag from Dominic's mouth, she mentally fished for a decent apology that would even begin to cover his ordeal.

"Hey, I know it's Christmas Eve and you were probably not expecting to be here right about now, and for that I'm truly sorry," she said, hoping he heard her sincerity.

He silently looked back, glared then stretched his jaw, the muscles in his neck flexing.

She immediately switched to the knotted rope on his bound wrists, then paused. "I understand you are upset, but how do I know you won't go ape-shit on me when your hands are free."

"I feel like going ape shit," his voice had always been hoarse and deep, but this was the first time she'd ever heard it filled with menace.

She stilled. "Ahh, wrong answer."

He inhaled and exhaled with calm precision. "Gin, even after all these years, you should know me better than that."

The old nickname was like an unexpected caress, a lick right at the nape of her neck. No one else had ever called her Gin except him.

"Not that Virginia is not a good name, but you need a nickname."

"Ginny. Everyone calls me that."

"No, I like Gin much better."

"I'm not an alcoholic beverage."

He'd paused. "Hmm. But you are something intoxicating."

"Oh, that's so corny." She'd rolled her eyes, but even as a teenager, his serious face and the youthful intensity in his gaze had stolen her breath as he'd replied. "I'm calling you Gin."

"Mr. Coscanos—"

"Come on." His smile was tight, but his gaze held her. "You used to call me Dom, remember?"

Oh yes, she remembered whispering his name between melt-in-your-mouth kisses…Double damn!

"I didn't ask for any of this, Dom, and I need some assurance that you will be civil if I set you free."

"If?" He threw a glance over his shoulder at her. "Didn't know having me tied and gagged was your thing, Gin."

She narrowed her gaze at him. "Maybe I removed the gag too soon."

He flashed a smile. "Whatever floats your boat, sugar."

This time, she did roll her eyes. "My point is that I didn't sign up for this either. If you can guarantee you'll be calm, I'll take the ropes off. Your choice."

After a tense scrutiny that seemed to drill right into her brain, he nodded and presented his back to her again. "I'd never hurt you, and I'm a little offended that you'd think it. My beef is not with you."

God, her brother was so doomed.

She hesitated, her gut tensing.

He gave her a sideways glance, his voice softening. "You are safe with me. I give you my word."

Closing her eyes briefly, she exhaled carefully then proceeded to untie him. Dom Coscano didn't know that she had kept her father's knife sheathed under the couch, another squirreled away in the bathroom closet and one more in the bedroom.

Besides, she still had her shotgun.

Once his hands were free, he turned to face her while he rubbed his wrists.

After an awkward pause, he went to the front door, opened it and stood outside. In the last ten minutes, the snow had gone from a blissful winter wonderland to something more blizzard-like.

"Well, Feliz Navidad," he grumbled under his breath.

Ginny grabbed her wine and stood in the doorway shivering from the cold. "I don't have a red-nosed reindeer, but if you want to brave the storm to get back to your family, you're welcome to my truck in the garage."

He turned to face her, weighing the option, then shook his head. "Weather is too risky."

"Your family owns a tow-truck company. One of your brothers would probably come by for you."

"They're all at my mom's house. And it would still be too risky."

Turning, they went inside and he unbuttoned his Santa jacket, taking out a small belly pillow to reveal a blue undershirt beneath. He looked like he was ready to get rid of the whole outfit, but instead reluctantly slid his hands into his trouser pockets in weary resignation.

"Your brother lost my phone. If you don't mind, I need to make some calls," he said.

"Sure." She pointed to the relic of a phone mounted on the wall by the kitchen. "Land line is best."

A few minutes later, she moved into the bedroom and changed her wet jeans for clean ones and found another pair of warm socks. Out of work habit, she threw the apron back on.

Dom was still standing by the kitchen, speaking rapid-fire Spanish to his family, and although she wasn't trying to eavesdrop, she did catch enough to understand that he was wishing them all a happy holiday and sending his regrets that he couldn't be there.

While he talked, Ginny checked on her dinner in the oven – their dinner, really. Before this whole mess, she'd been planning on a quiet evening, overindulging in wine and reminiscing over old photographs and memories that she planned to carefully unwrap like gifts.

Instead, the room had been robbed of its toasty heat from the fireplace, she was housing a reluctant and unexpected sexy guest – with whom she would have to share her Christmas dinner – and she was doing her best to avoid thinking of the night ahead.

What the hell was Brian thinking, dumping Dom at her doorstep? Did he ever give a second thought to her safety? Did Brian ever know how much it hurt her that he'd once again disrupted her life with another one of his messes? With every passing year, he seemed to become angrier and more self-destructive. It was getting to the point that she could hardly find a trace of her caring sibling any more.

Ginny set the table for two, trying to ignore the internal radar that told her exactly where Dom was in the room. Forcing her thoughts back to her brother, she worried whether he had made it safely to the freeway. Since she'd poured herself the last of the chardonnay, she held up a bottle of blended red wine to Dom for his approval.

With the phone still on his ear, Dom smiled and nodded, so she filled his wineglass and handed it to him. He sipped, mouthed a "thank you."

After he hung up, he stared helplessly at the phone, the picture of a Santa who was still processing the news that they'd found the shattered remains of his lost sled full of gifts, floating in shark-infested waters.

"I'm really sorry," she said, knowing it was hardly enough.

He shrugged, straightened. "As long as you understand that I'm pressing charges."

She held his gaze and nodded, feeling her heart getting heavy. "Fair enough."

He took a sip then said, "And I'm putting a huge chunk of coal in his stocking. And sizeable steaming reindeer turds, too."

She cocked her head to contemplate his mood. "He's got it coming."

His eyes warmed with amusement. "You're not going to try to talk me out of it?"

"Nope." She'd promised her mother she'd take care of Brian, but this last stunt was just too stupid. She was not going to bail him out any more, but the decision made her sad. "He made his mess, he can clean it up."

She turned back to the small kitchen to extract the roast from the oven, setting it to rest on the stove.

Behind her, he cleared his throat, and she felt the heat of his gaze against her spine. "Mind if I clean up a bit?"

"Go ahead. It's the first door on your left."

"Thanks."

<<>>

Dom stepped into the bathroom, switched on the lights and exhaled carefully.

Brian Parker deserved worse than a broken nose for kidnapping him, but there were worse things in life that being kidnapped and forced to spending a Christmas holiday with his high school crush, Virginia Parker. Until this moment, he'd been pretty sure than he could stand next to her and not have a tugging need to move in closer, to catch the scent of her perfume or revel in the way she pursed her lips in that dainty feminine smirk.

But no, she'd sank her hooks in him as a teen without even realizing it, and now, at twenty-two, she had mastered the sexy charm of just being a beautiful black woman. Back then, she'd been able to stun him with one glance of those luscious brown eyes. And she still had it. Just moments ago, when she'd smirked, he'd wanted to kiss her and hold her in an embrace that was seven years in the making.

That was definitely a problem. He faced his reflection in the mirror, spotting flecks of Brian's blood on his face.

He still remembered the day her parents had died in the horrible car accident. Within weeks, both her and her brother had been taken to another school district, to live with her grandmother. She'd stayed off social media, but he'd still been able to track her when she became her brother's guardian. And as other kids were going off to college, she had opened a bakery and began bailing her brother out of trouble on a regular basis.

For months after she'd moved, he'd tried to contact her, but she'd not returned his calls. Not once had she tried to stay in touch with him.

Dom saw his grin widen in the mirror and shook his head. Here he was with his old best friend, and among the swirling emotions was pure and simple lust. Damn, but some teenage fantasies never faded… He splashed water on his face, cleaning up and hoping to cool his thoughts.

Back then, there had been drama in the Coscanos household as well, with one of his brothers almost locked up and his youngest sister getting pregnant. His own problems had seemed too personal in the midst of all the shuffling family issues. One day, in frustration, he skipped class to ride his motorcycle over to Virginia's grandmother's house. He needed to talk to her as much as he needed to give his condolences.

At first, for a brief moment, she'd looked so happy to see him, but then, she put up a wall of aloofness between them. Almost without emotion, she'd explained that she had to be her brother's keeper, and that her grandmother needed help too. She was going to school but also working two part-time jobs. It was obvious she'd given the speech a lot of thought, and it all boiled down to letting him know she was cutting him out of her life, severing the past to tackle a new future.

"I understand, but maybe I can help with something, you know. Take you to the movies once in a while to get your mind off things—"

"I have no room in my life for movies, Dom."

"You're grieving, Gin. You don't have to go through this alone."

"I'm not. I've got my brother."

"What about friends?"

"Don't make it difficult, Dom. I don't want friends. I don't want romance. I just want to get on with my life. I'm sorry, what you want is complicated, and I really need to simplify. So this is goodbye."

No argument worked. Finally, anger and betrayal had goaded him back on his motorcycle. Pride kept him from glancing back at her.

He'd missed her for a long time afterward.

"Get a grip," he grumbled to himself. They had been different people then, and they were certainly different people now. But would she be open to a relationship now? Hope sprung ever-fucking eternally.

Straightening his shoulders, he opened the bathroom door and headed back, stepping quietly back into the kitchen to watch as she put the final touches on the dinner.

Understandably, in seven years, the quiet, shy girl had become a woman with serious, wary eyes and a familiar smile. She was certainly not rail thin any more, and there was nothing wrong with how the curves had bloomed and settled on her frame either. She used to straighten her hair, but now wore it in long thin braids that complimented her oval face. The rich, dark tone of her skin always had an enticing glow to it, as if she spent much of her time peering into hot ovens and bustling around her bakery.

She peered into the oven now, her loose braids swaying slightly, and her faded blue jeans and festive sweater making her look like she was no more than eighteen. But it was the way her apron stretched over her breasts where it read, "Santa gets his goodies at Luscious Cupcakes Bakery" that kept getting his attention.

He wondered if she realized what the writing said any more.

Mmm-mm, Santa's goodies indeed!

"So, how have you been doing all these years, Gin?"

There it was, that low rumble of his voice that even as a teen, sent delicious shivers up her spine, making her want to hear it up-close, within kissing distance. Maybe near her ear. Maybe against her skin.

"Fine." She flashed a smile and closed the oven door with more strength than she'd intended. "You?"

"Pretty good." From where he was leaning against the counter, Dom's stomach made a rumbling sound that surprised her and caused her to chuckle.

"Just a few minutes more. Dinner is almost ready and there's plenty of it. Do you mind grabbing some paper towels and bringing the wine?"

"Sure thing. I appreciate you sharing your meal with me," he said solemnly.

"Of course." She tugged off the oven mitts. "Merry Christmas!"

For a moment, they stood watching each other in an awkward pause, then he suddenly walked over to her small table and pulled a chair out for her.

As he stood there, waiting for her to sit at the table, the fireplace behind him, outlining him in a most inviting way… she couldn't help but think that he looked like he had been posing for a naughty calendar shoot… a sexy man who was done being nice, playing a jolly Santa, and wanted nothing more than to invite a woman to bring out the naughtier part of him.

"Gin?"

"Oh, yes." She hurried over and sat at the seat he held out for her. "Thank you."

"You're welcome." He sat across the table from her.

She smiled, hoping it wasn't as stiff as it felt and gestured to the food. "Help yourself."

A flicker of something heated flashed in his eyes before he turned his attention carefully to the roast beef. "Looks delicious."

For the next few minutes, they served themselves in relative silence. The music blended with the snap and crackle of the fireplace and the clinking of utensils against the dishes.

"Man, that's good," he said after taking a bite. "Wish I could cook like this."

Some of the tension eased from her shoulders. "It's easy enough, really. I found the recipe in one of my mom's boxes." Hell, why had she mentioned her mother?

He sipped the red wine, his eyes watching her closely. "Must be a tough time of year for you."

"No more than usual." She speared a carrot, casually waving it in a dismissive manner. "So, you were playing Santa at the hospital?"

He grinned slowly, acknowledging the change of subject with a nod. "It's for a good cause. The beard is obviously very fake ... and itchy... but the kids don't care. They love the Mexican and Italian Christmas carols and the gifts we bring. It's sad, but for some of them, this may be their last Christmas. They just want joy... and a break from being sick."

She quickly glanced down at her plate, embarrassed that her brother's convoluted plot had involved a children's hospital on Christmas Eve. Obviously Dom understood the worth of good will. "The Santa gig is a noble thing."

His gaze met hers. "Well, it's really not about being noble. I just want to be there when they need me, even if they are at their worst. Even if they think they'd rather be alone."

She focused on slicing her meat into a perfect square.

"I know it's water under the bridge, Gin, but I regret that I wasn't there for you all those years ago. I should never have let you push me away."

She shrugged. "I didn't need anyone. I just needed to move on. There was lots to be done and I had to be the one to do it. "She shrugged. "No time for silly teenager stuff."

The tines of his fork sank into a mushroom, pinning it to the plate. "There was nothing silly about our friendship. You knew how I felt about you. I knew how you felt about me. But you seemed lost in grief and–"

"Like I said, that's in the past, Dom. Water under the bridge." She took a sip of wine, letting him see in her eyes that she wanted the subject closed.

He held her gaze for several stubborn seconds.

"It is fortuitous that we ended up meeting again, huh?" He toasted her by raising his wineglass. "Here's to renewing out friendship."

For a moment, she hesitated with her wineglass half way to her lips. "Um, okay—"

"Relax, I'm still the same old me," his smile was just as carefree as when he'd been a teen. "How about you start by telling me about your luscious cupcakes, and I'll bore you to sleep with details about my accounting business."

The conversation unfolded easily after that. Amazingly, he made taxes sound interesting, and with his easy smile she found herself talking about the bakery, of how she loved to wake up early and start the dough, to open the doors to the street so the aroma baking would lure in clientele. She talked about the restaurants she supplied baked goods to, some of her quirky clients, and the satisfaction of knowing she was doing what she loved.

Feeling more at ease, she could see that his mannerisms were still the same. His Mexican-Italian heritage had blessed him with some seriously good looks. He gestured with his hands whenever he talked of something that excited him. There was a small dimple on the left side of his face that appeared only when he grinned. Despite her best efforts, it was a bit mesmerizing when it appeared. Obviously, time had changed him too. He seemed longer more than taller, as if his presence doubled, instead of simply gaining more height.

And his voice... oh, that voice.

They talked about music and movies, surprising each other by realizing they were still fans of the same football teams as in their youth. It felt like she was drinking him in, having a taste of the past but in a newer, refreshing way. It was certainly not the Christmas Eve she was expecting, but yet, it was going so well, she felt like a kid, staying awake to be part of the magic of the holiday.

Before she realized it, they had finished second helpings, almost emptied the bottle of wine, and were chatting easily.

"What?" she asked when his gaze locked with hers for a little too long.

His shoulders shifted in a light shrug, his smile still lingering. "This takes me back. We used to laugh like this when we hung out together, remember?"

She paused. "Yeah."

"I've missed this."

A soft, familiar loneliness tugged at her heart and she broke eye contact to start stacking the dirty dishes. "Yeah, well... that might just be the wine talking."

"It's not."

She glanced at him, but couldn't hold his gaze, so instead she carried the dishes to the sink. When she peered at him, he was scratching his chest in apparent discomfort.

Caught red-handed, he smiled sheepishly. "I'm dying to take this itchy jacket off."

"Go for it. You can take a shower, if you like—" She paused. "I mean, if you want to. I'm not implying that you shouldn't undress, because you can if you want to. I mean, you don't smell or anything..." Mortified with her ramblings, she momentarily closed her eyes. "Never mind."

When she opened them, he flashed a grin and wiggled his eyebrows, his voice ever so suave. "So what you're really saying is that you'd like me to strip off my Santa swag to the tune of these Christmas carols, is that right?"

She almost dropped the plate she was holding before remembering that he'd tease her in the same way as a teen.

"Say the word, babe, and I'll shake my moneymaker for you all night long," he continued. It was his salacious wink and chuckle that gave him away. "Watch out, Imma throw you some rhythm. Old-style holiday rap."

"Psht! Stop right there."

He cleared his throat, clearly ignoring her. "No pole, no sleigh. Just a personal ho-ho-holiday. Ch-cheer. Right here. Check out my Santa pants. Comes off when I lap dance. There's more to be had. Feliz Navidad. Not worries about the snow. Stay tuned for the show!"

Virginia couldn't hold back the burst of laughter. "Good thing you're a great accountant because rapping is not your calling."

He laughed too. "Ok, but all joking aside, I sure could use a shower. I'll give you free tax services for a decade if you let me wash this itch away. I'll behave. Scout's honor."

"You were never a scout."

"Wasn't I?"

She frowned, realizing she didn't really know.

"Okay, so I wasn't. But if I stay in this itchy suit, I'll definitely break out in a rash."

She turned her back to him and placed the dish safely in the sink, smiling to herself. "Fine. Go ahead. I'll get you a fresh towel."

He sang in the shower, and it was not any Italian piece that she recognized. It was probably a Mexican opera, since his mother loved to play that music. And he was in there. Buck. Naked. Showering.

And here she was, with a towel in her hands, just outside the bathroom door, waiting.

A completely wild and lusty thought bloomed in her mind and she couldn't let it go. What if… what if she didn't let this opportunity slide by? What if they could bridge the gap of seven years, back to the friendship they'd once had, to the attraction that still flared between them?

The singing temporarily paused for what she assumed was because he was washing his face in the spray of the shower.

What if she made the first move? This could be it! But did she dare? Was she brave enough to chance it? Hell, she still had those three condoms she'd bought on impulse back in July, back when she'd planned go to a bar to find a lover for a carefree, one-night stand. That hadn't happened. Sure, she'd always had feelings for him, but this was no different, right?

Heavens, was she crazy?! She'd just met him again after a seven-year gap. What if having sex with her hadn't even crossed his mind? What if he was engaged to someone? Or he couldn't because of some hideous penis affliction?

The bathroom door opened a crack and she almost jumped out of her skin. A partial view of Dom's face, chest and hip was visible, glistening in the dim light while a puff of steamy air moved past him and kissed her face. She couldn't look away from a drop of water that moved down his jaw, trailed over the angled muscles of his neck and –

"Gin?"

She swallowed, her gaze snapping back at his. With a pressed smile, she held the towel out.

"Thank you." His eyes gleamed, seeming to read so much more than she wanted him to. As soon as he took the towel, she turned on her heel and went back to the bedroom. Clothes. What the man needed was clothes, and soon.

In the top section of the bedroom closet her brother kept some clothes, most of which would probably not fit Dom. But if she remembered correctly, Brian had some big baggy pajamas that he'd complained about but hadn't thrown out. Maybe those would do for now.

"Hey, Gin?"

"In here. Just getting you some pajamas."

She sensed the minute he entered the room, her pulse racing when she turned to watch him approaching, towel wrapped around his hips. She tugged hard at the pajamas in her grasp, realizing too late that the small pile of clothes that sat on it was tipping over her head.

Somehow, he got there a half second too late, but with enough time to put his arm out to deflect more clothes from bouncing off her head.

"Damn," she mumbled, looking directly at his chin, mere inches away.

Time stretched as the seconds piled up. His lips formed a faint smile. "Did you say Damn or Dom?"

"Damn."

"Remember the last time we made out?"

She stiffened. "Dom, don't bring that up."

"We were in a closet at Martha Sandoval's birthday party. Shoved in there for a full minute by our so-called friends."

"Yes, yes, yes. Spin the Bottle or something stupid like that. Your point?"

His gaze touched her face, intently, stealing her breath with each passing second. "It ended too soon."

She'd been embarrassed and nervous. "This is ridiculous! Let's just pretend and get out of here."

For a very long second, they just watched each other.

"You ready?" he finally asked.

"Ready?"

He nodded. "Yep."

She paused to think about it. "That's been long enough. Sure."

She had been expecting him to lead the way out but instead, he cupped her face and placed a tender kiss on her lips, teasing and tasting as if he was drinking.

Stunned, she'd parted her mouth, and taking advantage, he angled their mouths and made it a real kiss.

She'd been spellbound, smitten, living a dream. Every time their lips parted, she whispered his name.

The loud bang of someone's fist against the closet door jarred them back to reality.

Realizing what she'd done, she'd stormed out of the closet before she could be dragged out by her friends.

The memory brought a blush of embarrassment mixed with anger. "Your pajamas are somewhere on the floor."

"Thanks, "he drawled, his other hand coming up so that he each hand braced on either side of the wall by her face. He leaned in to whisper in her ear, almost touching it. "So, you ready?"

A fissure of desire unraveled deep inside her when he his large hand came up to cup her cheek, shifting down to the pulse at her throat, angling her face just slightly toward his to that their eyes locked. "Yes or no, darling."

Dear God, he was going to kiss her! And if he didn't hurry up, she wasn't sure she would not faint. "Yes."

Her eyes slid shut as his lips touched hers. It was not the tender, teenage kiss she'd dreamed of. This was a devastating, delicious kiss, full of pent-up hunger and passion that was pulling at its reins. It was dominating and demanding, and she found herself matching him, clutching his head and shoulders, no longer light-headed from yearning, but rather empowered to seduce, to indulge and take as much as she could handle.

"Gin, Gin," he murmured against her cheek, before making a sexy, rumbling sound deep in his chest, and kissing again. She moaned in delight, easing against him with aching need.

He pulled her close and time lost meaning. His hands moved over her hips and buttocks, rolling their hips together, his arousal swelling and growing more insistent between them. His mouth nipped her chin, his tongue licked and tasted the nape of her neck, and the world felt like it tipped dangerously on its back.

When his hand slid under her sweater to cup her breast, she shivered and moaned his name.

As if waking from a dream, she realized he'd more or less frozen in place. His breath was still billowing against her cheek, and his hand twitched slightly where it cupped her breast, but he held still.

"Honey, we're going too fast."

Still breathless, she struggled to make sense of his words. "Hmm?"

He nipped her bottom lip as if he couldn't help himself. "God damn... I want to make love to you more than anything else in the world, but ... we're still almost strangers and I don't want to assume anything or take advantage or—"

"Dom, please." She'd meant for it to sound like "Please stop talking" but instead, the breathy urgency in her voice had made it sound like "Please, oh please, fuck me."

"Woman, you're killing me," he growled, dropping a very demure kiss on her lips.

She sank her fingers into his head of hair and clenched. "You asked if I was ready. Well, guess what? I really am. And I know we just met, and we're both adults but if you're having second thoughts–"

"Querida, after all these years, I've never been able to get you out of my head, and I don't want to mess this new thing we have now. I want you." His hand caressed her breast, his erection remained a steady hard heat against her jeans. "But I don't want to rush things with you—"

She held his head to give it a light shake. "All's fair if there are no regrets, right?"

He grinned and murmured something in beautiful flowing Spanish. "Hmm?"

"I can't wait to undress you. "He placed a butterfly kiss on her cheek. "And taste every inch of you that I've dreamed of." Another kiss. "And I'll make you breakfast in the morning."

She chuckled in delight. "Are you going to talk a lot during sex?"

He growled and in a fluid move, lifted her in his arms, stepped over the clothes and walked a short distance to lay her down on the bed.

"Please tell me you have condoms," he said.

"Three!"

"Anywhere near here?"

"In my purse." She hated to leave his arms, but she rolled away from him to hunt through her purse on the kitchen counter for the condoms.

When she had them, she paused and fanned herself, nervous and thrilled with the knowledge that Dom was just a room away, hers for the night. Deep inside, she knew she'd be happy talking to him all night, but this? Maybe she was being reckless, but it felt like something more, like a gift.

Impulsively, she stripped down to her bra and underwear, the delicate pink material contrasting against her dark skin. Mingled in with the faint scent of cherry blossom lotion that was still on her skin, was the scent of her wet arousal. With the three condoms in hand, she returned to the bedroom to find Dom lying under the flannel sheets.

He raised himself up on an elbow, his face full of clear admiration. "You cheated! I wanted to undress you."

"I left you a little somethin'. Are you saying you don't want to?" she teased.

"Mmm, I'm thinking I wouldn't mind watching you remove the rest of your clothes yourself."

She tossed the linked condom packets at him, and they landed on his chest, his attention never leaving her. In a very amateur move, she tipped her head back and tossed her thin braids to cascade over her head, then shimmied her hips and ran her hands over her breasts, moving her fingers up over her nipples, her shoulders and lowering the bra straps.

He sat up in the bed, the condoms sliding off his chest.

Feeling suddenly shy, she unhooked her bra, quickly slid it off and tossed it at him. He caught it and brought it up to his nose, his nostrils flaring as he inhaled, still watching her.

"Aw, sugar, come here-come-here-come-over-here. Right. The hell. Now!"

"What about my panties?" she teased.

When she saw that he was about to come for her, she rushed to the bed, jumping on it to pin him down, but instead he rolled her beneath him, the contact of skin on skin causing the playful mood to transform into something more. "Gotcha."

He kissed her deeply, touched her eagerly, but reverently, each caress drugging her breath and stripping her thoughts into nothing but taste and touch, sight, scent and sound.

It was so erotic to feel that lovely, dark, rough tone of his voice against her skin, whispering words she didn't understand, to get caught in the storm of passion that he seemed to control so easily.

She arched against the flannel bed sheets, allowing him access to her to her panties when he tried to remove them, feeling the unique, hard heat of his erection as their legs tangled to push the panties down her legs and off her ankles.

The world turned and she was rolled above him, her breast within easy access to his mouth. She moaned at the feel of his teeth and tongue teasing her aroused nipples while his hands spanned her hips, thighs and butt.

The world tipped again and she was on her back, her mouth being devoured hungrily while his hand eased down her waist to the junction of her thighs.

Oh, Jesus God!

Possessively, his palm covered her there, his fingers gathering her arousal and stroking her sex with it, two fingers sliding in, inch by inch, repeating until she was moaning and hyperventilating.

"Dom?"

"Si? Tell me what you want, what you like…"

She did, with her moans and barely murmured words, moving against him, again and again almost reaching a peak that promised delirium.

Finally, at her wit's end, she clutched his hand to keep him from driving her insane. "I need," she gasped. "I just need," she repeated, then kissed him. "Need you now."

It seemed like one minute she was trying to catch her breath, and the next he had the condom on and was leaning over her, gently pushing back some braids from her face to kiss her. Positioned between her thighs, he guided his cock into her, the tip alone feeling so much bigger than his fingers that she stiffened.

"Easy, querida," he slowed, eased back out and kissed her until she was loose and achy again.

He kept up the slow seduction until she had a sheen of sweat on her skin and was wriggling beneath him.

She ran her hands over the span of his back, brushing her ankles against his calves and shuddering at the sensation of another shallow thrust, craving more. He seemed determine to torture her, moving slowly, gently, rocking against the tight entry.

"Dom," she groaned, biting him gently on the neck.

"Too tight." His eyes slid tightly shut in concentration, sweat dotting his brow.

She wrapped her legs over his buttocks and arched into the next thrust, enduring the intense tightness and sudden pain.

His eyes sprung open, locked with hers as understanding dawned. Freezing completely, halfway inside her, he barely managed to ask in shock, "You're a virgin?"

"Yes." She rocked into his thrust, taking him completely, deeply, and so fully it was uncomfortably tight and overwhelming. But the sharp pain began fading quickly, to be replaced by an age-old urge to have him return the thrust.

"Ahhh..." Every inch of his body tensed and his teeth gritted loudly as he clenched them. "Don't move, love. Dios mio."

After several sacred seconds, his arms repositioned around her, cradling her.

"Dom, please don't stop," she whispered urgently.

He groaned, but thrust ever so carefully.

If the pace before had been slow torture, it now became intensely more, gathering its own exquisite momentum. Giving over to her instincts, she matched every one of his thrusts with her own, riding the sensation that was building inside her to a spot that was so different from her clit when she masturbated. Almost mindless, she shifted underneath him, angling his cock toward that magic spot until she was clutching his shoulders and tensing against the growing waves of sensation.

"Ohhhh, Oh, oh!" The climax hit like a jolt of electricity, clenching deep in her gut and returning in pleasurable waves, tingling like shimmering ice crystals on her skin. She shivered and trembled, taking pleasure from his final hard thrust that made him grunt and shudder above her.

The aftermath was like floating on a calm surface after having being dragged and tumbled underwater. She coasted on the sweet, serene silence, the weight of his body shifting against hers, skin and sweat mingling, the half-trust enough to remind her of her loss of virginity. Looking like a fallen warrior, Dom's head came up, his eyes searching hers with worry. "Virginia."

"Hmm?"

"How do you ...feel?"

She smiled lazily. "Divine."

"Divine? What does that mean. Gin, you're wrecking me."

She kissed his chin. "Honest, it was better than I was expecting."

He tried to pull out, but she tensed her legs over his thighs, this time she watched him closely. "No regrets, right?"

"None," he said solemnly. "I wish I would've known though. I'd have done things a little differently, been more patient."

She felt herself blushing. "There are still two condoms left."

He grinned, watched her in fascination for a long moment as he ran his fingers over her cheek in a gently caress. "Why didn't you tell me?"

She shrugged. "Hey, I didn't ask you if you were a virgin."

He raised an eyebrow. "Good point. But you know what I'm asking. Why now, why me, after all these years?"

"I, ah..." never felt about anyone, the way I did with you. "I felt comfortable with you."

He glanced away for a split second. "It's Christmas time and you're lonely, huh? Comfort and convenience?"

"No." She grabbed him by the chin. "No, please don't think that! I've dated other men, and wished I could feel more with them, to take the relationship to an intimate level. I've had several comfortable and convenient opportunities, but I just could not go through with it, believe me. It's just how I feel, and not something I can rationalize or compromise. I couldn't lose my virginity to any man because it would've been convenient. I just … I never felt the way you made me feel, Dom. I mean…" To her surprise, she could feel emotion thicken her words. "And I'm not saying that to put any expectation on you—"

"Oh, hush, Gin."

"Please let me finish. I just want to say thank you—"

He made a sound of frustration and something else.

"—and as crazy as it sounds, given the circumstances of how you ended up on my doorstep, I am glad you are here with me tonight. I feel so, I don't know, lucky."

"Lucky?"

"Maybe that's not the right word. But to be totally honest, I don't have the right words. I just have a bunch of emotions that feel like I've been given the best Christmas gift ever."

A tender, intense expression came over his face. "Okay."

The more the watched her, the more self-conscious she felt, so she winked, trying to lighten the mood. "You did a phenomenal job. Yay, Santa!"

He groaned and shook his head. "If you try to tip me and send me on my way, there's going to be big trouble."

She ran her hands over his wavy hair. "Dom, I just don't want you to feel that you suddenly have an obligation to me now or anything like that."

"Hush, it's my turn. "His gaze narrowed and the frustration was back on his face. "You may not know this about me, but I don't do one night stands. So, my sexy lover, you should know that I, on the other hand, do feel an obligation, as you call it. In fact, I consider us to now be in a newly-minted relationship. We did things a bit ass-backwards, but I plan to fix that. There's going to be dinner dates, movies, and I'm ever-hopeful for a quickie at your bakery."

The emotions in her chest seemed to be multiplying. "Just one quickie?"

He sighed, pretended to think about it. "I'm open to negotiations. "Then he placed a soft kiss on her lips and became serious again. "You blocked me out of your life years ago, Gin. I understand why you did it. I do wish you would've told me you were a virgin, but I'm not letting you go again. Not without a fight. Do you object to any of that?"

His gaze held hers and she could see that he meant every word.

"No objection."

"Good."

He placed a kiss, sending her heart spiraling again. Oh, my heavens, my feelings for him are on him full force! The blooming sensation in her chest felt too full, aching like a secret that refused to be suppressed.

For a long moment, they stared at each other like happy fools, until she finally said, "Mind if I take a shower?"

"God, I'm an idiot." He eased off her, looking like he didn't know what to do next. "Yes, of course."

She started to get up, then looked at him over her shoulder. "Want to join me?"

For a moment, a tender, possessive look fleeted over his face. "I'd love to."

<>>

Dom spent several pleasurable minutes covering Gin with soapy suds, taking the opportunity to caress her, to drink in her reaction to each touch, and kissing her until she was wiggling against him.

"Not now, querida. Let's wait for a bit. Don't want to make you too sore."

"Aw," she grumbled. "If you're not going to deliver the goods, don't tease."

He chuckled and pulled her into his embrace, letting the cooling water wash over them. Did she have any idea how he felt? He wanted her to obsess about him, to care as much as she cared about her remaining family. No. That was duty. He wanted her to care for her with a passion only she could understand. The way she loved...

"Cupcakes. Think cupcakes."

"Cupcakes?"

"Sure, thanks. Nice of you to offer. I'd love some."

She laughed and splashed him with water. "Fine. Only because it's Christmas, and I didn't put milk and cookies out for Santa."

"As the official Santa, I'd be honored to have your cupcakes and kisses anytime, sugar."

She looked up at him as if she wanted to say something more, her eyes guarding her thoughts.

"Gin, I'm only asking to make cupcakes because it will be something I can do with you other than ravish you like a sex-starved caveman."

She rested her forehead against his chest, then peered up at him. "Me Jane. You Tarzan?"

"I've created a monster." He laughed, turning off the water and grabbing a towel for both of them, trying to nudge his erection into compliance. "I'm trying to be a gentleman. And I want to make something fun—"

"Sex is fun!

"–like cupcakes!"

"Sex and cupcakes?"

He groaned and his nostrils flared with desire.

"Okay, maybe you're right," she conceded. "Let's go make some cupcakes."

He made such an effort to restrain himself that Virginia decided to humor him and put on her pajamas, then hurried to change the bed sheets. He tried on the pajamas she'd found for him, but the top was too tight, so he went bare-chested, which was absolutely wrecking her concentration.

"I thought you said two cups of flour?" he said, as she placed the ingredients into a bowl.

She reluctantly looked away from his manly, hair-sprinkled chest to check her measuring cup, realizing she'd overfilled it. "Oh, well, I did that was to see if you were paying attention."

"I have outstanding laser focus."

"As do I, but maybe I should be shirtless too and we could test your focus some more."

He paused, stared at her shirt as if he could see through it, then walked around to stand behind her, putting his arms around her to get to the mixing bowl. "Never mind, I have a better idea. We can work like this. Less distracting for you."

She wiggled her butt against his front, grinning at how his body immediately responded. "This flannel is a little bit hot."

She began unbuttoning the pajamas until it hung open.

He pushed some of her braids aside so he could nibble her ear. "If you're trying to break my focus, it won't work."

He placed a kiss on her neck, then without a word began to measure milk to add to the bowl.

"Stir it slowly to incorporate all the ingredients." She arched backward ever so slightly. "You want them to mingle just right."

He barely held back a grunt. "Butter?"

"Oh, yes."

He place some into the bowl.

"Save some for the icing."

"Mmm. My favorite part."

He patiently followed step by step, until the tray of six cupcakes were ready for the oven.

He cupped her butt when she bent over and placed them in the oven, then, as soon as the door was closed, spun her around, his lips hovering over hers. "You mentioned icing?"

She felt like she was running a fever. "Mmm-hmm."

"Teach me, Gin." His lips barely brushed hers. "Show me what goes into that wickedly tasty stuff."

She nipped his bottom lip. He kissed her hard, and making her knees weak. They broke gasping for air. "Dom?"

"Love the way you say my name like that," he confessed, making an effort to keep their lips from touching. "Now, about that icing…"

"What about it?"

He spun her back around. "Let's make some so I can focus on … something else."

With him pressed closely behind her, they mixed butter, powdered sugar and some brown sugar, cream, vanilla and cinnamon until it was the perfect consistency and she was ready to scream.

He dipped his finger into the bowl and tasted it with a hum of appreciation. "Delicious. How was my focus?"

"Annoyingly impressive." She held his hand back into the bowl and brought it to her lips to suck and lick, nipping the pad of his index finger. The creaminess was perfect, and the brown sugar granules gave it a lovely texture. It was worth the exercise in focus just to see his eyes almost slide shut with lust.

When she released his finger, she grinned slyly, challenging him with a raised eyebrow. "Santa like?"

"Very, very much."

He lifted her and placed her on the kitchen counter. Behind her, she heard a whisk fall to the ground, but Dom was fast enough to catch the bowl of icing when it started to slip away.

Like a magician, he pulled apart her flannel pajama shirt, her breasts rising and falling with each excited breath. With an expert touch, he took some light pink icing and spread some on each dark nipple, pressing and rolling the tips slowly enough that she could feel the granules of sugar against the sensitive skin.

A tightness began coiling inside her with each caress, making her feel vulnerable and naked as he watched her enjoying the caresses. But when he lowered his head and took her breast into his mouth, the tightness uncoiled into a shudder of pleasure that made her sway slightly. "Oh! Oh my…"

With masterful precision, he rolled each of her nipples with his tongue, those granules creating a yearning ache when they pinched slightly, building the pleasure as he licked all the icing off. His hands roamed, his skin touched, and their mouths met, tearing up more kisses until the oven timer dinged loudly.

Showing more control than she had, he stepped away to turn the oven and timer off, then returned to pull her off the counter. Grabbing the icing with one hand, he lead her to the couch by the fireplace.

The towel still lay on the arm rest, so he spread it on the seat, and leaned down to kiss her belly button as he pulled off her pajama bottoms. When they slid off, he parted her thighs and inhaled deeply, bracing as if in pain. "That scent… and the icing… holy God, Gin. Incredible."

Although she was equally aroused, she fought a sudden shyness. "I-I should get the condoms from the bedroom."

He lifted his head, his gaze filled with tenderness. "No. I'll take care of you. I promise. Lean back, close your eyes and enjoy the ride." She hesitated, then complied.

It was devastating.

He painted icing on her inner thighs, her navel, and with one finger, painted icing rosettes around her sex. Satisfied with his design, he proceeded to drive her completely crazy by rubbing in the icing, licking, eating and sucking every last bit off it from her skin, focusing on her swollen clit and simultaneously stroking every part of her sex with his fingers. She moaned and shivered, blindly needing more, caught up in the storm of sensation as his tongue swirled, suckled and stroked her until she came hard, hips shifting off the couch a bit, vaguely aware that her right hand was clutching his head to the juncture of her thighs until the last waves of pleasure faded.

For a long moment, he knelt there, his face lifting and resting against her thigh. The fire crackled for another long while the afterglow faded enough for her to realize that his breathing was still choppy.

"Dom?"

"Si, querida?"

"Are you okay? Shouldn't I do … something?"

He used a corner of the towel to wipe the shine of sex from his face, his eyes still gleaming with repressed lust. "I just need a moment."

With the fireplace behind him, he looked so capable and sexy, the feelings for the man before her far surpassing the teenage crush for the boy he'd once been. Everything he had done made her feel special, cared for.

She caressed his cheek, realizing he was still trying to be a gentleman. "I know you didn't finish. I wouldn't mind, you know, taking care of you too."

His smile grew to a grin, and he turned his head to kiss her palm. "I should be saying hell yes, but to tell you the truth, I could stay here at your feet, just to watch you like this for about an hour."

Moved beyond words, she unconsciously moved a hand over her heart and smiled.

Time seemed suspended until the shrill of the phone cut sharply into the room, jolting them both. One look, and she could tell that, like her, the only person that came to mind that would call was her brother.

"I don't want to talk to him," she said.

"You should." He nodded toward the offending instrument. "Maybe he finally came to his senses."

It rang one more time before she leaned over, placed a kiss on Dom's lips, then went to answer the phone, picking it up without a greeting.

"Hey, sis? Sis?"

"What?"

"Okay, first of all, I'm sorry! I know I fucked up. I'm so sorry. I just want to know if you're okay? Please tell me you're okay?" She held the phone away while he continued. It was easier to watch Dom with his stubborn erection, go into the restroom and hearing him washing his face.

"Sis? SIS?"

Virginia reluctantly brought the phone back to her ear. "Glad you made it safely back to town, Bri," she snapped. "Mom would be so proud."

He paused. "Fuck. Yeah, I know Mom and Dad would've kicked my ass."

"When are you going to grow up and stop doing shit like this, Brian?"

"I was trying to do a good thing, honest."

"I have better things to do than listen to your excuses, Brian."

"I know. I didn't want to bother you, but Tommy made me call. I mean, I was going to call anyway, but Tommy said I should call right away and apologize."

Saddened that he'd actually needed prodding, she didn't say anything, and the silence between them stretched.

"I was honestly trying to do something right, you know," he finally said. "I know it wasn't, but... once I knew it was Dom, I figured it was fate in a way. I remember you guys together back in high school. You were in love. Everyone knew it." He sighed, paused again. "Last New Year's, when I showed up late at your house for the flashlight, remember? You were drunk and were falling asleep on the couch, crying a little and saying his name over and over. I'd never seen you drunk before, sis. I mean, I know he's special to you. So, like I said, it's almost like fate, right?"

"Oh, Brian." She remembered drinking too much on New Year's, when she'd been expecting to celebrate alone, but loneliness had driven her to overindulge in alcohol. "None of that justifies what you did."

Dom stepped out of the bathroom, his erection having abated a bit. He walked toward her and pointed at the phone. "Mind if I talk to him?"

She handed him the receiver. She could hear Brian stumbling over his apologies all over again.

Dom interrupted. "Do you know how many women I've slapped in my life? How many I've cut up, tied up or used against their will? The answer is none! But you didn't know that when you dropped me off here. Had I been someone else, this stunt of yours could've backfired ten ways to Sunday! I could've killed your sister or done so much worse! I don't think breaking your skull is going to knock any sense into it. But you'd better believe that if you ever pull another stupid stunt that puts your sister's life in jeopardy again, you'll have me to deal with."

Brian responded with something she couldn't decipher.

Dom again interrupted. "I don't waste my time with empty threats, Brian. It's a promise. You'd better figure out how to make this right with your sister, and do it soon or we're going to have a whole new conversation. Right now, at the count of three, you should wish your sister a Merry Christmas and hang up."

This time, she could clearly hear Brian yelling out, "Merry Christmas, sis. I'm really, really sorry! I do love you!"

Dom handed her the phone.

She held it tightly, suddenly feeling like she betrayed the promise to her mother in some irrevocable way. Saying goodbye to her brother seemed very final, as if she'd turned a corner in her relationship with him. "Merry Christmas, Brian. Goodbye."

"I'll talk to you in a few days, okay?"

Sadness turned into a knot in her throat. "Mmm-hmm."

"Thanks, sis. Again, I'm so sorry."

She waited to hear the dial tone before hanging up.

Dom opened his arms, and she stepped into his embrace, wordlessly accepting the comfort she never realized she'd needed.

"So, for New Year's, I think you should come and meet my family," Dom said.

They were mired in the afterglow of lovemaking, this time in the bedroom on fresh sheets. She was snuggled up to his ribs and he was lazily playing with her braids.

"You don't think it's too soon?"

"No. I gave up seven years that I need to make up for." He placed a puff of a kiss on the top of her nose. "I'm trying not to rush things, but if you need me to slow down, please tell me. I want to be with you, Gin. I think we could be good together. Good for each other, to each other."

She smiled tentatively. "I feel the same way too, Dom. But can you honestly say you'll feel the same way next week?"

"What? Do you think I'm only in it for the sex?" He paused, frowned, then spoke softly. "Are you telling me you only want sex?"

"No!" She touched an index finger to his chin, making an effort not to blurt out the word 'love' and throw herself at him. "I'm just telling you that the sex is pretty darn good, but I'm new at this and I don't want you feel like you have to feed me some line."

"It's no line, Gin. It's how I feel. How do you feel?"

She took in a deep breath, looked into his eyes and spoke from her heart. "I feel if you respect me at all, tell me if you only want the next few days, or if you truly want more."

He grinned. "Absolutely, positively more. You have my word."

She bit her bottom lip while grinning. "Yeah?"

"So, let's pretend it's been six months, and you're still crazy about me."

"I'll be certifiably insane."

"And I am still deeply and madly in love with you."

Her heart thundered and a gasp escaped her. "Oh, Dom."

"Don't cry, sweetheart," he murmured when her eyes watered. "You don't have to say you love me back right now, just know that I do love you, right here, right now. No doubt in my mind about that." His lips brushed hers. "So, anyway, if you feel warm and fuzzy about me in six months, would you marry me?"

"Dom!" She could no longer hold back the tears of joy. She threw herself at him, covering his face with kisses and holding him close. "I do! I will! God, yes, I'll marry you! I've been trying not to blurt out that I love you and make a fool of myself, because I know you care about me, but I wasn't sure if—"

The kiss he planted on her bloomed like a promise. Words, thoughts and emotion sealed between them in a kiss that took her breath away.

When they finally broke for air, he breathed, "I love you, Virginia."

"Love you, too, Dom," she said, emotion choking her words. "And Happy fricking Feliz Navidad to you, sweetheart."

He hooted and rolled her around with her on the bed. "Absolutely my very best Christmas ever!"

ABOUT THE AUTHOR

I've always loved reading romance novels, and I feel so lucky to be an author who can share my own plots and characters too. I took a hiatus a few years back, but my muse calls, so I'm doing a bit more writing these days.

Feel free to browse my other books on my website: www.delil ahdawson.com and let me know what you think.

I love to hear from my fans, so if you want, drop me a note a ddawson@delilahdawson.com. Thanks!"

FIRE AND FRUITCAKE

EILEEN RENDAHL

Clara pointed at the candle in the middle of the menorah – the shamash, the one you use to light all the others – and flame burst from its wick. She clapped her little starfish hands in delight. I licked my fingers and pinched the candle out, glancing around to see if anyone else had noticed.

"Mamamamama," Clara chanted, a frown pulling her lower lip down.

Uh oh. The last thing I needed right now was for her to go into full-blown tantrum mode. We were pushing our luck as it was. It was already six-thirty. Based on what I'd seen of the latke production happening in my mother's kitchen, we would not be sitting down to eat until close to seven. Clara was usually in her bath about now, followed by cuddly story time, then sleepy time by eight.

And yes, I'd heard in my head what I sounded like. I wasn't sure what frightened me more: the kind of language that motherhood was making me think in or one of Clara's epic meltdowns that seemed more likely to happen when we threw her schedule out of whack. As a Messenger, I have fought off Chinese vampires, rogue werewolves, evil brujas, and more. I have gone toe to toe with gnomes, trolls, and chupacabras. I would be willing to take them all on again rather than endure my daughter's ear-piercing shrieks during one of her arched back to hell and gone tantrums.

Now I had to contend with the possibility that she might decide to go all firestarter on the menorah in front of family members who didn't know or understand about me being a Messenger. Or her being … well, whatever she was. None of us were quite sure about what that was yet.

I scooped Clara out of her highchair and settled her on my hip. "Why now, pumpkin? Why tonight?" I considered asking her why tonight was different from all other nights, but that question goes with an entirely different holiday than the one we were celebrating tonight at my mother's house. We were in full Hanukkah mode. Passover was months away.

Before Clara had been born she'd shown signs of having an electric personality. She'd let off shocks here and there in utero, mainly to protect me or her father. Mainly her father. All that had stopped when she was actually born. Which mirrored what had my mother had told me about when she was pregnant with me and when I was born. Except then I'd fallen into the pool at age three, nearly drowned, and woke up a Messenger.

Clara had been a regular baby so far. She cried, ate, slept, and pooped. A lot. That was it, though. No sudden shocks. No zapping. Then tonight when we walked into my mother's dining room, she saw the candles, pointed at one of them, and poof! Literally, poof! This was seriously not good.

"Let's go find your Daddy." Maybe Ted could distract her while I hurried things along in the kitchen. Maybe we could get out of here without having a heck of a lot of 'splaining to do to the family members who didn't quite know what I was besides awfully lucky to have scored such a nice husband and such a cute baby despite my somewhat surly personality.

"Dadadadada," Clara agreed, curling her fingers around the neckline of my shirt. I gave her tiny fists a kiss – yes, she was starting fires, but she was still the cutest bestest baby in the whole world – and went in search of my husband (it still felt so weird to even think of him like that) and her father, Ted Goodnight.

I found him watching basketball with my father and brother in the den. I caught his attention and gave him a little head jerk to indicate

I needed to talk to him alone. He followed me out of the den and toward the sun porch at the back of the house.

"If you're trying to foist another dirty diaper on me, I want you to know it's not cool," he said taking Clara from my arms. "Just because you can smell it before I can doesn't give you license to dodge your share of changes."

I didn't point out that the fact that I could smell it long before anyone else was often punishment enough. "You're going to wish it was a dirty diaper," I said, checking my shirt for spit up or any other body fluids. "She pointed at one of the Hanukkah candles and it lit up."

Ted looked from me to Clara and then back to me. "Like in flames lit up?"

"Like totally in flames lit up."

As if to prove me right, Clara chose that moment to point at a votive candle my mother had on the windowsill and light it on fire. I licked my fingers again and pinched it out. At this rate, I was going to need to develop asbestos fingers.

"This could be problematic," Ted said.

"You think? What if she decides she doesn't want to nap and sets her crib on fire? What if she decides she doesn't want to share and sets another kid on fire?" The what ifs mounted in my brain like debris from an avalanche. Motherhood felt like that a lot. Like a whole mountain of crap was coming toward me and all I could do was stand there and try to make sure it didn't get in my mouth and eyes.

"Let's keep calm. So far she's only lighting up things that are supposed to get lit up, right? Think of how handy that'll be on camping trips." He leaned in and kissed my forehead.

"I don't camp." It's not that I didn't see the appeal of starry skies and fresh air, I just also had to contend with whatever supernatural creatures made their home wherever I was trying to sleep. It didn't make for restful nights under the stars. Besides, what was so bad about indoor plumbing?

"I know. Imagine it hypothetically." He grinned at me, making it nearly impossibly to not at least smile a little back. He was awfully cute with that messy blond hair and big blue eyes and ridiculous dimple, all of which he had passed on to our daughter. Did I mention that she was the cutest bestest baby in the entire world?

I still wasn't happy about our little bundle of joy becoming Miss Sparky, though. "We're going to have to do something."

"Like what?" Ted sat down on one of the wicker chairs my mother had placed looking out onto the garden and bounced Clara on his knee.

"No idea. I'll have to ask around. Somebody somewhere must have dealt with a baby firestarter before." We couldn't be the first, could we? There had to be some kind of precedent somewhere. Please let there be a precedent somewhere.

"Of course they have." Ted nodded. "I'm sure we'll find several chapters in a Dr. Spock book on firestarter training. Maybe there's a What to Expect When You're Expecting a Fiery Conflagration?"

"You're not helping." My phone buzzed in my pocket as my mother sang out that dinner was ready. Finally. "You take her in. I'll be in in a second. Try not to let her set anything on fire."

The text was from Dawn Bianchi. Dawn was a forensic veterinarian at the University who'd gotten caught up in a situation with a werewolf-hater when a dead werewolf ended up on her autopsy table. Diego, another werewolf, and I had tried to get the body before she got too curious, but the whole thing kind of backfired. Instead of making sure she didn't get involved we wound up with her dating Diego and spending her free time stitching up werewolves and a few other creatures.

Her text read: Something weird at my lab. Can you come see?

I answered: Are you in danger?

Her response was: Srsly? That's how you think I tell you I'm in danger?

There were reasons I liked Dawn. Sarcasm was definitely one of them. I answered: Tomorrow okay? Around 10?

In response, I got a thumbs up and a smiley face. I went to have Hanukkah dinner with my family.

Clara was eight months old. She had two teeth. My mother's brisket was so tender that she was able to eat it. Just saying.

Hanukkah overlapped Christmas this year, as it does on occasion. We'd spent the morning before with Ted's mother. Clara had been delighted with ripping wrapping paper off packages, playing in boxes, and eating cookies. Ted still wasn't totally okay with his mom suddenly being back in his life. She'd abandoned him and his father when he was a kid, leaving him alone with a mentally ill parent. Or possibly not mentally ill. I thought it was possible that Ted's father might have been at least part Arcane and that it had been his own powers that had driven him mad. It explained a lot of things, things about Ted. Like why he always smelled like cookies to me and how he always found fantastic parking spaces. Norah claimed there was nothing in her grimoire about cookie-scented parking place-finders, but I was convinced there was more on heaven and earth than was dreamt of in the grimoire Mae had given me for my twelfth birthday.

The next morning, Clara ate her breakfast and played without setting anything on fire. She didn't even torch anything when I was buckling her into her car seat, something she often protests by arching her back, twisting, and pulling her legs up so I can't fasten the straps. Maybe we'd be okay. Maybe she wouldn't set things on fire when they irritated her. That could happen. I could get lucky for once.

We drove over to the vet school to see Dawn. This visit was a far cry from the first time I'd been in Dawn's lab. That time, Diego and I had shimmied up the side of the building and in through a balcony door on the third floor that had been left unlocked and had kicked the door to the lab in. It was way easier to come in through the front door, give my name at reception, and walk down the hallway, especially with a baby on my hip.

Well, I had a baby on my hip for about ten seconds. Dawn practically snatched her from me. "Hello, Princess. How are you today?"

I stretched as we walked. I was developing a permanent crick in my neck. "Well, she hasn't started any fires today so I'd say it's a good day so far."

Dawn cocked an eyebrow at me. "Is that new?"

I nodded. "And not entirely welcome. I'd rather she started swearing."

We got into the lab and Dawn handed Clara back to me. "So what do you have?" I asked.

"I'll show you." Dawn gestured to a sheet-covered mound on her autopsy table. "Is she going to be okay seeing this?"

"I guess we'll find out." I shifted Clara so she was looking back over my shoulder just in case.

Dawn pulled back the sheet to expose a charred blackened vaguely human-shaped lump. A small human-shaped lump. Without thinking about it, I clutched Clara closer to me. "Is it a child?"

Dawn shook her head. "I don't think so. Based on the teeth and the skull and the long bones, it was full grown, whatever it was. It also had a tail and horns. That's how it ended up here. The medical examiner was pretty sure it wasn't human. I'm pretty sure it's not an animal. Or at least not a mundane one."

I was starting to understand why she'd called me. "Where was it found?" Clara wiggled against the tightness of my arms. I sat down on Dawn's desk chair and let Clara slip into my lap.

"Site of a house fire over in Boulevard Park. Looked like their Christmas tree went up like a Roman candle while they were up in Tahoe skiing." Dawn drew the sheet back over the creature.

"A Christmas tree fire? I thought those were an urban legend." Or at least historical legend since pretty much no one put real candles on Christmas trees anymore.

Dawn sat down on the rolling stool by the table. "Maybe it's the drought. It's possible the tree was dry to start with. Or there was an electrical short. However it happened, this thing was underneath it when it did."

"Bad timing." I certainly understood all about being in the wrong place at the wrong time. It had been the story of a good deal of my life.

"Bad lots of things. Like taste. Based on its stomach contents, it was gorging on fruitcake." Dawn wrinkled her nose.

Definitely weird. I didn't know anyone who actually likes fruit-cake. Well, anyone American. I have some wacky Scottish friends who think that stuff is the bomb. "How quiet can you keep this?" The last thing any of us Arcane beings needed was a bunch of Mundanes getting their holiday undies in a bunch over whatever this was before we determined if it was even bunch-worthy.

Dawn said, "Half the University is closed. I think I can keep it pretty quiet."

That was good news. "What about the medical examiner?"

Dawn thought for a second. "He's a busy dude. I'll try to come up with a cover story before he checks in. Meanwhile I'll write this guy up as too damaged to classify."

"Good." I gathered up Clara, fist-bumped Dawn, and headed to the car. On the way there, I called my former roommate and still best friend Norah. "You feel like coming over for dinner?"

"I don't want pizza."

I knew she wouldn't. I also knew I had exactly what she wanted. "I have leftover brisket from my mother's."

"You're on. What should I bring?"

See? I knew my bestie. "Your grimoire."

Next stop for Clara and me was the River City Martial Arts Studio. I inherited the dojo from my sensei and Messenger mentor, Mae, when she died fighting off the kiang shi, a type of Chinese vampire. I run it now with the help of my Messenger protégé, Sophie. I didn't know what I'd do without her. She was smart, independent, responsible. If I'd had half as much on the ball at eighteen as she did, I don't know where I'd be now. Possibly right where I was, but who knows?

We generally shut the studio down between Christmas and New Year's. Too many people were out of town or wanting to spend time with their families. Rather than teach half-full classes, we used it as a chance to do a big clean. When I got there, Sophie had all the doors propped open and was already pulling up mats.

I set Clara in the corner in a horseshoe-shaped cushion I kept there, surrounded her with toys, kicked off my boots, and pitched in.

"You know, you're not going to be able to do that forever." Sophie gestured at Clara with her chin. "She's going to start to crawl soon and then what will we do?"

I glanced over at Clara. She was rocking from her butt up almost onto her knees, plopping back, and then clapping for herself. "We're going to enjoy this phase while we're in it and pray she doesn't set the place on fire."

Sophie folded over a heavy section of mat and started to roll it. She was only about five foot five and thin. She had that extra little burst of Messenger strength, though. Between her slight frame and the waves of blonde hair, the super strength surprised a lot of people even though she was fairly adept at keeping it from showing too much. Besides, a lot of people were too busy looking at the burn scars on the side of her face to take proper notice of her.

Sophie had been in a terrible car accident when she had been thirteen. She'd almost died. Kind of like how I'd almost died when I was three. Then somehow – poof – we were both Messengers. I'd never been given definitive proof that the whole near death thing was how we ended up with our powers, but it seemed like an awful big coincidence.

I didn't believe in coincidences.

While we rolled up mats and surveyed the state of the floor beneath them, I filled Sophie in on what Dawn had shown me.

"What is it?" she asked.

I kicked at some dirt that seemed stuck to the floor. "I really don't know. Norah's bringing her grimoire over tonight. I'll see what she can find in it."

"But it's already dead, right?" Sophie used the momentary break to stretch, pulling her arm across her chest.

I nodded.

"And nobody seems suspicious, right?"

I nodded some more.

"But you're worried anyways?" She folded over into a toe touch.

I kept nodding. It wasn't that I liked to borrow trouble, I had plenty of my own without taking in loaners. It just seemed little problems

44

like these ones often became big ones that were a lot harder to take care of. "I want to make sure I have a handle on whatever it is that's going on. Just in case, you know?"

"Got it, boss." Sophie wiped the dust off her hands. "This enough for today? I thought we could start the serious scrubbing tomorrow."

"Sounds perfect." Anytime anyone suggests I stop cleaning, I make sure to agree.

"Okay if I stop by tonight, too? Just to make sure I have a handle on what's going on, too?" She smiled. "I could bring soda."

I smiled back. She was going to be such a better Messenger than I was. "Of course."

I reached for the grimoire, but Norah pulled it out of my reach. "Hand over the brisket first."

I pushed the platter toward her. It's not like I couldn't get more. I could actually make my own. I mean, my mother had given me the recipe. Unfortunately, it required two things I was generally short on: time and patience. The not-so-secret to my mother's recipe was cooking it low and slow. That and onion soup mix.

Norah took a helping that was probably twice as much meat as she'd eaten in the past two weeks and shoved the grimoire to me. "Look at the page I marked."

I shoved it back at her. "How about you give me the low down? What do you think this thing Dawn has is?"

She put down her fork and dabbed her mouth with a napkin. "A Kallikantzeroi."

"Gesundheit."

Norah rolled her eyes. "Very funny."

She opened the book to the page she had bookmarked and took another bite of brisket. I'd given Norah the grimoire back when she'd first figured out that the beings I regularly carried messages for weren't all blue fairies and benevolent brownies and proceeded to fully freak out on us. To avoid having a constant sprinkling of salt on all the windowsills while she cowered in a corner of her bedroom, I gave her the grimoire. I'd never been much to study it and she found a little knowledge about what was around her all the time to be more calming than terrifying. "Seriously, a Kalli what?" I could barely read the spidery writing on the page.

"A Kallikantzeroi. They're Greek. They spend all year sawing at the roots of the World Tree, but get a vacation between Christmas and Epiphany. They come to the surface and by the time they go back down, the World Tree has healed itself and they have to start all over again." Norah started eying the container of leftover latkes.

"They do this every year?" I opened the lid and let the steamy potato-y goodness scent the air.

"Every year." She put two latkes on her plate and layered on the applesauce and sour cream. Hanukkah might be the only time Norah ate dairy. She made more dietary exceptions for the Jewish holidays than she did for anything else. Sometimes I worried that she was more Jewish than me. Not that that would be all that difficult. "They haven't figured out that they need to skip the annual vacation to achieve their goal of … what? What is their goal? What happens if they actually saw through the roots of the World Tree?"

"Destruction of the world as we know it, I believe, and no, they haven't figured it out. They're not the brightest bulbs in the supernatural chandelier." I read a little bit in the grimoire. "According to this, you can completely stop them by putting a colander on your doorstep. For some reason, they're compelled to count the holes, but can't count higher than two."

"So what are you going to do about it?" She pushed her plate back. She might love Hanukkah food, but she was only as big around as a toddler's pinky finger and it wasn't hard to fill her up.

I picked Clara up and set her in her high chair. "Nothing."

"Nothing as in no action at all?" She got up and kissed Clara on the top of her head.

"Yup. You got it. Nothing gets by you, does it?" I put some shreds of brisket on the high chair tray, then a few bits of latke. Clara picked up the baby spoon I had set on the tray and banged it.

"Then why the research?" Norah asked.

"Because it's not a good idea to decide to do nothing until you know that nothing is the right course of non-action." I tried to spoon some applesauce into Clara's mouth with a second spoon. She grabbed that spoon from my hand and banged it on the high chair tray.

"Kallikantzeroi are a nuisance. Nothing more. The one that Dawn has was in the wrong place at the wrong time."

My cell phone buzzed before I finished my last sentence. I picked it up from the counter.

It was another text from Dawn: I've got another one.

Crap. Ignoring the dead Kallikantzeroi was starting to seem like less of a good option.

I left Clara with Norah and went back to the vet school. No receptionist this time, but I still didn't have to climb the wall to the balcony. I texted Dawn and she came right down.

"So what exactly are these things?" Dawn asked as she led the way back to her lab.

I explained the basics of the Kallikantzeroi to her. "Is this one burned?"

Dawn shook her head. "Decapitated."

"Eww."

She shrugged and unlocked the door. "I'll take that over road kill any day. Much less messy."

"Anyway it could be accidental?" I knew that sounded desperate, but a girl could hope, couldn't she? If it wasn't accidental, then the crispy critter version most likely wasn't accidental either. If neither of them was accidental, something or someone was running around killing stupid Canes and I was not sure I could ignore that. I have this idiotic weakness for standing up for the downtrodden even if the downtrodden deserved to be trod.

Dawn shook her head. "I don't see how. Whatever did this was sharp. Whoever did this had quite an arm. You don't sever someone's spinal cord with a tap from a butter knife."

"Did this one come through the medical examiner's office, too?" It would be better if the world of Mundanes did not know too much about our dead friends, regardless of whether or not the deaths were deliberate or accidental.

"Nope. A grounds crew found it. They thought it was weird, but were too grossed out to look too closely. They saw the tail and the horns and called Animal Control. Animal Control brought it to me." She pulled a metal gurney into the center of the room.

"Lucky for us." I would take whatever breaks I could get.

"Totally. Because otherwise I'm not sure how I would explain this one away." She pulled off the sheet to show me the two pieces of Kallikantzeroi that lay there. I would not have looked too closely if I could have avoided it either. If this guy was representative of his species, the Kallikantzeroi were not pretty beings. He – and it was definitely a he – was a weirdly crabbed little thing with a long tail extending behind him and horns jutting out of his forehead. Not only was he ugly, he also stank.

I held a hand over my face to block the smell. Dawn seemed totally unaware of it. "Where was this one?"

"Under a Nativity scene on the St. Ignatius campus." She recovered it with the sheet. It blocked the sight, but not the smell.

I could not quite picture where that was. "Where is that in relation to the Christmas tree fire?"

Dawn pulled a map out of one of her desk drawers. "Let's see." She grabbed a pen and circled an intersection and then another spot about an inch away. "There and there. About a mile from each other. Is that significant?"

"Maybe. What else is near there?" I wanted to pinpoint where they were coming up. It might help me figure out who was slaughtering them.

Dawn let her fingers linger on the map. "Kind of everything. It's all near downtown. Why?"

"They have to be coming up somewhere. They don't burrow through the earth. They use established pathways. I hope it's not the tunnels under Old Sac again. I have some seriously bad memories about those." I shivered remembering the way the Kiang Shi had risen from beneath the Buddhist temple. They'd been dug up accidentally during a renovation project that had accidentally broken through into the tunnels. "Are there any big construction projects near there?"

Dawn turned and stared at me. "Have you been living under a rock? Have you heard of a little thing called the Golden 1 Center?"

The Golden 1 Center was huge. It was the site of the new Sacramento Kings arena plus venues for concerts and shops and restaurants. That extensive of a construction project could create any number of pathways, tapping into existing routes and creating new ones. I sat down. "That would do the trick. Anything else I should know?"

"I'm not sure this means anything, but it was weird. Remember how I told you the first Kallikantzeroi's stomach contents were made up of fruitcake? Well, this one was clutching half a fruitcake and it looked there was a trail of fruitcake leading to where it was found."

According to the grimoire, Kallikantzeroi loved fruitcake. It's like Kallikanternip. "Someone lured it there."

"Like an ambush?" Dawn asked.

I did not like that I was thinking it, but there it was. "I don't know, but it looks like a possibility, doesn't it?"

"But who?" she asked. "Why?"

"Excellent questions." Too bad I didn't have any answers.

When I got back to the apartment, the joint was jumping. Ted had gotten home from his shift. Alex had stopped by to help Norah with her babysitting duties, Paul had come over, and Sophie had shown up.

I looked around the room. "Norah ate all the brisket. There is none left."

Alex rolled his eyes and I couldn't help but smile. As a vampire, he didn't really eat food the way we did. Or, more to the point, we were his food. Well, Norah was. It was not something I wanted to think too much about, but it actually seemed to do her good. She basically glowed all the time these days. Paul was not really a candidate for the meat my mother cooked for hours and hours on end either. Werewolves tend to like their meat rare, even when they're in human form and the meat isn't. Ted was most likely the only one who was disappointed and he had had plenty the night before.

"Is Clara asleep?" I asked.

Norah nodded. "She nodded off about eight."

"Perfect," I said. I sank down onto the floor and looked around the room. It was good they were all there. "Listen, I think we may have a problem."

They all listened as I filled them in on the two Kallikantzeroi Dawn had found.

"You think they're coming up through the Golden 1 Center?" Paul stood up. "Let's go then."

"Go where?"

"To. The. Golden. One. Center." He enunciated each word as if I was dim. Which maybe I was because it hadn't occurred to me.

Ted, Alex, Paul, and Sophie all started putting on their jackets. "Wait. What about Clara?" I asked.

"I'll stay," Norah said. "But it's going to cost you."

"What's your price?"

She crossed her arm over her chest. "Some of that chopped up fruit stuff. The stuff that's supposed to be like mortar, but is mainly just delicious."

It took me a second to figure out what she meant. "You mean charoset?"

"Yeah. That's the stuff. The kind your mother makes with the dates and the apricots." She nodded happily.

"Wrong holiday. Charoset is for Passover, not Hanukkah." Norah might make dietary exceptions for Jewish holidays, but she still never could keep them straight.

"Fine, then. What else is traditional for Hanukkah?"

I thought. "Jelly doughnuts? Really anything fried. That whole miracle of the oil thing."

She shook her head. "Nope. I want the fruit stuff."

What could it hurt? "Fine. I'll see if I can get my mom to make some." "Then you have yourself a babysitter."

I looked at the chain link fence that surrounded the Golden 1 Center construction site. It wasn't too high. I could make it over easy. Post-pregnancy I was a tiny bit slower than I'd been in my prime and my center of gravity was off a little bit. Still, it would take a lot more than a ten-foot fence to keep me out.

"Do you think there are dogs?" I asked Paul. For whatever reason, dogs hated me. I though they sensed that I wasn't what I seemed to be on the surface.

Paul raised his head and inhaled deeply. "Don't think so." Then he smiled and started making chicken clucking noises.

"You wouldn't think it was so funny if they chased you," I said.

"Good point. Want a leg up?" He cupped his hands for me to step into.

Ted stepped between us. "If my wife is going to step on any of us, she's going to step on me."

"Suit yourself, man. She lose all that baby weight?" Paul grinned.

"I lost enough of it," I snapped. Seriously, why did they always talk about me like I wasn't there? Oh, yeah. I remembered why. Because they knew it drove me nuts. It was like working with a bunch of thirteen-year-old boys sometimes.

I stepped into Ted's cupped hands and vaulted myself over the fence. I didn't exactly stick the landing, but it was graceful enough. "The rest of you coming?"

Ted came over next with an assist from Paul, then Alex, then Sophie with Paul on her heels.

"Now what?" Sophie asked.

We all stopped and reached out with whatever senses we had to see if we could locate any Kallikantzeroi. Then we pretty much all started choking.

"What is that smell?" Alex asked.

I braced myself and gave a little sniff. It was the same smell that had been in Dawn's lab. I hadn't smelled it on the first Kallikantzeroi, probably because it was too badly burnt. "I think we've got a live one."

"What smell?" Ted asked.

"The one that smells like dozens of teenaged boys put their sweat socks into a giant stock pot and stewed it with some milk that's gone bad and seasoned it with something dead," Sophie said.

Ted shook his head. "Yeah. Not getting that at all."

"Consider yourself lucky." Although if Ted couldn't smell it that might explain why the construction workers weren't running off the job site with their eyes streaming. Maybe that was why Dawn hadn't seemed bothered by it in her lab either.

We picked our way through the darkened area. I glanced over at Ted to see how he was doing. Everyone else had enhanced night vision. It's one of the perqs of being a Messenger, or a werewolf, or a vampire. Not so much one of the perqs of being a cute cop. He glanced back at me and winked. I was relieved. I didn't want him tripping and falling, but I also didn't want him using a flashlight. The less attention we attracted, the better.

"This way," Paul said. He'd taken the lead, which made sense. He was, after all, arguably the best hunter among us, which was saying something. He turned right to go deeper into the site.

"Oh, by the way," I said as I followed Paul. "Don't let it get on your back."

"Why?"

"You'll have to carry it around all night while it talks to you."

"Thanks for the heads up."

"My pleasure."

The smell got stronger. We had to be getting close. Then I smelled something else. "Does anyone else smell … fruitcake?"

Paul stopped and we looked around on the ground. Ahead of us was a trail of chunks of sweet bread with those weird fake fruit chunks. "Where does that go?"

"One way to find out," Ted said and started following it, again heading deeper into the construction site.

"Maybe we should follow it the other way, too? See where both ends of the trail go?" Sophie suggested.

"Hard to know. I figured it was best to just pick one end and go with it," Ted said.

Alex snorted. "That explains a lot."

My eyes narrowed. "Really? You think now is an appropriate time for that kind of teasing?"

"One thing I have learned in my vast number of years upon this earth is that it's almost never the right time for anything so you might as well do what you want when you want." Alex walked after Ted.

I hurried after him. "So exactly how many years is that vast number?" Alex has never told me how old he is. Vampires have extremely long life spans. They're hard to kill unless you're specifically trying to vampire slay and most people aren't.

"Long enough, Messenger. Keep moving," he said over his shoulder.

I trudged behind them. I pulled part of my shirt up over my nose to mask the smell. Ted was lucky.

We came to an area where a pit was being dug. The sides went straight down approximately twelve feet. The whole pit was probably fifty by fifty. Over in one corner of the square, there was an area that had crumbled away. "Do you think they could be coming up through there?" I pointed.

Paul sniffed. "Yeah. I do."

"So what do you think is at the other end of the fruitcake trail?" I asked.

"I'm pretty sure there's only one way to find out." Paul tilted his chin at the trail.

He was right. "We should leave someone here to guard the entrance in case one of them comes out."

"I'll stay," Sophie raised her hand.

"I'll stay with her," Ted volunteered.

The rest of us started back along the fruitcake path. "So here's what I don't understand," I said. "Why? Why do this? These things are only nuisances. Why go to the trouble of trapping them and killing them when all you would have to do is set out a colander?"

"Maybe we'll find out at the end of this trail of fruitcake," Paul said.

I giggled. "There's a sentence I bet you thought you'd never say."

"Since I've met you, I've said a lot of sentences I never thought I'd say." He didn't sound angry about it, though.

"What kind of sentences?" I pushed.

"Melina ..."

"Seriously, what kind? Lovey dovey sentences? To Meredith?" I made my voice all sing-songy.

"Melina," he said, his voice a little more urgent.

"Paul and Meredith sitting in a tree ..." I sang.

"Melina!" Paul's voice was sharp.

Sometimes werewolves were no fun at all. "What?"

"Stop talking and pay attention. Do you sense anything?"

I stopped, froze really. I closed my eyes and let my other senses take over. There was something there, something terribly faint. I looked up at Paul and nodded. "It's 'Cane, but not very 'Cane."

He looked around, eyes narrowed. "I got the same thing."

We swung around to look at Alex.

"Smells a little like food to me," he said. Vampires didn't feed on other supernatural creatures. Their tastes ran pretty much only to human blood.

"How far?" I asked.

"Up ahead, around that corner." Paul pointed.

I didn't see anything. "Do you think it knows we're here?"

"Maybe. It's being awfully still," Paul said.

"So maybe we should proceed with a little more subtlety and subterfuge?" Alex said, his head cocked to one side.

I accepted the rebuke. I deserved it. The three of us melted into the shadows. I was pretty sure I could only make out Alex because I knew he was there. Paul was a little easier to spot, but still difficult enough to find to fool most human eyes. We moved through the stacks of lumber and pieces of large equipment on feet that were nearly silent.

There was a scraping noise. Whatever was ahead of us had finally moved. I caught Paul's eye and he nodded. I skirted around a stack of metal beams and saw the end of the fruitcake trail. I held my hand up to stop the other two from coming any farther. Whoever was out there – and there was someone and not something out there – didn't need to know how many of us there were.

I skirted around the open area where the trail ended. I could hear breathing now, harsh and scented with fear. I guessed that it knew I was there, but didn't know exactly where I was. Advantage: Melina.

I took a few more steps and it – or should I say he – bolted. I felt a breeze as both Paul and Alex took off after him, but seconds later I heard the sound of a car engine and knew the chase was off. They were fast, but they weren't car fast. Sure enough, they came trooping back a few minutes later.

"He got away." Paul looked like he might pout.

"I gathered."

We walked back along the trail to Ted and Sophie.

"Did you get a license plate?" Ted asked when they'd told him the story.

Alex smiled and rattled off a series of numbers and letters.

Ted pulled out a notepad and jotted it down. "I'll look it up tomorrow at work."

"Any sign of any Kallikantzeroi?" I asked.

Sophie shook her head. "I didn't see or sense anything."

I blew out a breath. "Let's head home. Maybe this will make more sense tomorrow."

That was when the smell went from bad to hellacious gag-worthy fetid worse. "There!" Sophie cried, pointing to the corner of the pit. A small dark figure emerged, tail whipping energetically behind it.

Paul jumped down into the pit. "Got it," he said.

"Paul, no!" I shouted. "If it gets on your back you'll be walking all night."

He shrugged. "I could use the exercise." He knelt down so it would be easier for the creature to climb onto his broad shoulders.

Even from this distance, I could barely stand the stench. "How are you going to be able to stand it?"

Paul laughed. "Motherhood has made you soft, Melina.

Clara was an early riser. Surprise! I mean, what eight month old wasn't, right? I was spooning mashed bananas and cereal into her adorable pink mouth when my cell phone buzzed. Paul.

"You're alive?" I asked.

"Just. Can I come up? I'm on your doorstep."

I hit the buzzer and waited by the front door. His steps dragged up the stairs. "You've looked better," I observed as he came into view.

"I've smelt better, too." He plucked at the shirt on his chest. A funky miasma rose from it and assaulted my nose.

I pulled the collar of my shirt up over my mouth and nose. "Truth. Maybe you should shower before we talk."

"It's all over my clothes." He looked pained.

No way was that kind of funk going to wash out. At least, not enough for Paul's and my sensitive noses. "Maybe you should burn them."

"You have anything I could change into?" There was a hopeful glint in his dark brown eyes.

Paul was taller and broader than Ted, but sweats stretch, right? "We'll find something."

Paul started stripping down as he walked into the apartment. Seriously, werewolves have no modesty whatsoever.

I rolled my eyes. "Dude. Not in front of the kid."

"Or my wife, please." Ted walked into the hallway stretching.

The smell became overwhelming. Clara made a face and started to whimper. I put my hand over my nose and mouth. "Never mind. Just Get those things off and let's get them out of here."

Ted took Paul's clothes down to the Dumpster while I finished feeding Clara and getting her dressed for the day. Ted had coffee made by the time Paul got out of the shower. He looked like he was about to burst out of Ted's sweats, but it was better than smelling like a Kallikantzeroi. "So what did you find out?"

"I found out a lot. Herb is quite the talker." Paul picked up Clara and bounced her on his lap. She giggled and grabbed his beard.

"Herb?" I asked.

"Yeah. The little guy. His name is Herb. What? Did you think they didn't have names?" Paul picked Clara up and blew a raspberry on her tummy. She shrieked with joy, kicking her little legs and waving her fat little arms like a wind-up toy.

I hadn't actually thought about it. "Fine. Herb. Go on."

"Anyway, the parts that actually are pertinent to us are like this: somebody's been picking them off one at a time since they started coming up on Christmas Day night. Some of them have been lured places." He settled Clara back onto his lap, his face suddenly grim.

"Like with the fruitcake?" Ted asked.

Paul nodded. "Some have been followed. Some have been killed as they came out."

That set me back on my heels. It was bad enough when I thought two of the little stinkers had been killed, but apparently those two were only the tip of the Kallikanter-ice berg. "Do they know why?"

"Not a clue. They're not the sharpest claws on the paw, but they're sharp enough to figure out that they're in danger." He rolled his shoulders.

And now for the six million dollar question. "Do they know from whom?"

Paul shook his head. "From what Herb described, it's a bunch of 'Danes. No magical powers. No super strength. Just 'Danes."

"'Danes that know Kallikantzeroi exist. That's got to narrow the field." I chewed on my lip.

"To what? Every person of Greek descent in the Sacramento metropolitan area?" Ted asked.

I shot him a look. "I didn't say it would narrow it a lot. Just that it would narrow."

I bumped the jogging stroller down the stairs of the apartment building with Clara on my hip. Once I got to the sidewalk, I strapped her in and we took off for the park. I didn't run as far or as fast as I used to, which quite honestly was fine with me. Running was one of those things that I always wanted to have done, but didn't want to do.

Right after Clara was born, I'd had the excuse of not wanting to jostle my lady bits anymore than they'd already been jostled. Eight months later and that excuse no longer held water. Plus, a jog through the park seemed to be the easiest way to get Clara to nap. Apparently all that stuff about fresh air was actually true.

The tule fog had started to lift, but the edges of everything still looked soft and blurry. I tucked the blanket a little higher under Clara's chin and zipped my jacket. The chill would feel good in a mile or so. Right now it made me want to turn around and go back to bed.

I tried to vary my route. There was nothing more dangerous than mindless routine, but there were only so many directions to go jogging in Mansion Flats. So I also tried to keep my guard up, especially when I had Clara with me. Precious cargo and all that, right?

We made it to the park and started weaving our way along the bike path. We were only a few yards in when I felt the prickle on the back of my neck. And this was a full force prickle. Not the tiny needle sticks I'd felt at the construction site. I slowed to a walk. Chances of me being able to outrun whatever it was were wafer thin, especially while pushing a jogging stroller. Trying to would only be a waste of energy and quite possibly make us into even more inviting prey. The thing about hunters was that they actually liked to hunt. If you run, they'll chase you even if it's just for entertainment.

"I need to keep moving," I said to the air. "Otherwise she won't go down for her nap."

Even though I was braced for something, the chittering noise down by my ankles made me jump. I looked down. A humongous squirrel leapt along the side of the path. Ratatoskr. What the hell was he doing here?

"Good morning, Messenger."

I was surprised at his snotty tone. After all, he was a messenger, too. He wasn't even a messenger with a capitol M. He spent all his time running up and down the world tree, otherwise known as Yggdrasil, carrying messages to and from the eagle that lived at the top of the tree and the worm that lived beneath it. "Good morning to you, too, Ratatoskr." I sounded downright pleasant in comparison to him, which said something about how rude his tone was.

"I have a message." He started to pick up his pace.

I broke into a jog. "For whom?"

"We're not sure." He leapt up onto a bench and ran along its back.

"We?" I panted. "Who's we?"

"Me. My friends at the top and bottom of Yggdrasil and the Kallikantzeroi." He kept leaping along, bushy tail straight up behind him.

"So your World Tree is the same as the Greek World Tree?" I gasped out.

He stopped and sat down, bright little black eyes looking at me. "How many freaking World Trees do you think there are?"

Frankly it wasn't a question I'd pondered in the past, although in my experience sharing wasn't exactly the strongpoint of anyone in the supernatural world. That was part of the reason I was even needed. If everyone could make nice with each other, there'd be nothing for me to do. They could carry their own damn messages. "Okay, then. You share. Gold stars all around."

"So here's the thing. The Kallikantzeroi are talking about going home early since it's not safe for them here." He sat down on his haunches.

Seemed like a reasonable solution. "And that's a problem why?"

"If they go back early, the World Tree won't have had time to heal properly. They might be able to saw through it if they started early and it was still damaged." He shook his furry head. "Duh."

That was a problem.

At that moment, Clara clapped her hands, pointed at a Ratatoskr's tail and it burst into flames.

That was a problem, too.

Ted went on duty at three. At four, he called me. "The car Alex saw is registered to a Kappas Construction."

A construction company truck at a construction site? Not exactly fishy. "Could it be somebody checking on the site? Have there been any other crimes in the area?"

"The timing seem suspicious and then there's all that fruitcake ..." I heard Ted tapping at his keyboard. "A lot of vandalism complaints. Mainly of holiday decorations."

"That has to be the Kallikantzeroi. Ripping apart holiday décor is one of their specialties. But why would this Kappas fellow want to bring the whole world down? What purpose could that possibly serve?" I never understood why villains wanted to destroy the whole world. I mean, didn't they have to live in it, too? It seemed way too much like a cartoon character taking a saw to a limb he was sitting on.

"I don't think he wants to bring the whole world down. He's not messing with Kallikantzeroi anywhere else except right around Golden 1."

"So he hates basketball? He's a Warriors fan? What?" It still didn't compute as far as I was concerned.

"No. Think about it, Melina. He's in construction. What if he wants to destabilize the area a little. Maybe cause a few cracks in the roads or shake the bridges a bit. Who gets hired to fix those things? I think he's guaranteeing himself work for the next decade."

Would someone be that venal? That greedy that they would risk other people's safety for their own profit? That they would actually kill other beings to set up a ploy like that? Who was I kidding? Of course someone could be exactly like that. The kind of someone who would use a bunch of stupid 'Canes to do his dirty work would totally be like that.

"So what do we do?" I asked.

"I think we have to keep the Kallikantzeroi safe until it's time for them to go home." The answer was so Ted. Protect and serve and all that.

"That's over a week! How are we going to do that?" I am so not Ted. Or even Tedly for that matter. It was part of the Yin Yang glory of our relationship.

He hummed while he thought. "Isn't the dojo closed for the week? They could stay there."

I didn't like the direction this was going. "We're supposed to open up again right after New Years Day. That leaves us with five more days to cover."

"Send out an email. Tell everyone you found mold under the mats and need extra time to get rid of it. Everyone hates mold."

And so Operation Kalli-Capture began. First we needed bait. I called my mother.

"Mom, do you have any fruitcake?"

"I have the two loaves cousin Lynn sent to us and to your grandmother this year. Why?"

"Can I have them?"

"For what? Some kind of gag present?" She snorted. "And I mean gag literally."

"No. For, uh, something else."

"Something … Messenger-y?" She paused. "Do I want to know?"

Mom knew about me being a Messenger, but there were some things she seemed not to want to know about. I didn't blame her. Most of the time I didn't want to know about them either. Case in point? Stinky little Greek demons whose whole goal in life was to destroy the world who now somehow needed my protection so that the world didn't get destroyed. I considered. "Maybe after it's all over. Until then, I think you probably want to stay out of it."

"Are you in danger? Will Clara be okay? What about Ted?" Wow. I was at the top of that priority list. I'd sort of assumed Clara would come first.

I got a little misty thinking about the fact that my Mommy loved me. Would those pregnancy hormones never fully leave me? "We'll all be fine."

"Then you're welcome to the fruitcake. You know, it's possible that last year's are down there as well."

"Fabulous."

I gathered up Clara and headed over to Mom's.

In the chest freezer in the garage, there were two loaf-shaped foil-wrapped items in the corner. I pulled those out and dug a little farther and came upon two more. I kept digging. And digging. And digging. By the time I got to the bottom of the old chest freezer I had ten frozen fruitcakes. Figure half a loaf to lure a Kallikantzeroi into the van. I had enough to lure and trap twenty of them. How many could there be coming up through that particular pathway?

I came back into the kitchen. "Mom? Can I borrow one of your colanders, too?"

"Same reason?"

"Yep."

She sighed and pointed to the cabinet. "Be my guest."

I took two.

We reconnoitered that night at the dojo.

"Okay." I looked around at the assembled faces. "What do we have?"

"I have four fruitcakes I gathered up from my mom and cousins, but I really hit the jackpot at the after Christmas sales. I picked up sixty of them for about a hundred and eighty dollars." Norah gestured out at her car. "I'll need some help carrying them in. Those suckers are heavy."

"I'll pay you back," I said. Norah had a good job, but nobody wants to throw around nearly two hundred bucks.

"From what? Your special Messenger Reimbursement Fund?" She snorted. "Like that exists."

It didn't. I'd still have to find a way to pay her back.

"I have ten," Paul said.

"I have eight." Ted dumped his on the table.

"My grandma had three." Sophie set hers next to Ted's.

Alex said nothing. We all turned to look at him. "Fine. I didn't get any. I was busy and I don't eat so nobody gives me food. I'm the one who got the license plate. Doesn't that count for anything?"

He had a point. "Fabulous. That should be plenty to lure them and still some to feed them with once we get the to the dojo. Are we ready?" Everyone nodded. "Then let's go."

I scooped up Clara and started toward the door. No one followed.

"Uh, Melina?" Ted said.

"What?" I asked. "We've got the van, the fruitcake, the colanders. What else do we need?"

"Do you really think we should take Clara?"

I froze. I'd gotten so used to doing everything with a baby on my hip, I hadn't even considered it. "I'm not sure we have a choice."

"How about we drop her at your mother's on our way downtown?"

I hung my head and texted my mom. She was waiting on the doorstep when we pulled up. She scanned over the group. "Does this have to do with all that fruitcake?"

"Yes."

She held out her arms. "Come to Grandma, Clara. We'll have a grandma/baby sleep over. Pick her up in the morning." With that she turned and shut the door in my face. Maybe I wasn't at the top of that list.

Downtown was as deserted as it had been the first time we'd visited the site. Still, we made sure to park the van on one of the side streets. Paul used a bolt cutter to cut through a chunk of the fence and remove it while I shimmied up the streetlight pole to break the bulb. We didn't need or want light for what we were about to do.

Ted and Alex stayed at the van while Paul and Sophie and I made our way to the pit, leaving crumbled pieces of fruitcake behind us like some sort of bizarre Hansel and Gretl gone wrong. We were about halfway there when I sensed something. I turned to Sophie. "You feel anything?"

She lifted her head and shut her eyes. "Not really. Why?"

"You?" I asked Paul.

He stopped and sniffed. "Humans. Let's hurry."

We broke into a run. There were three men at the edge of the pit, each one had a fruitcake and were laying a trail like we had. "I'll take care of them," Paul said, already stripping off his clothes.

If you had never seen a werewolf change, it was impossible to take your eyes off it. If you had seen a werewolf change a dozen times or more, it was still pretty difficult to not stare. It was fascinating. The way their faces elongated and their limbs shortened. The way their backs bent and haunches formed. There really wasn't time to stand around and appreciate Paul at the moment, though. I nudged Sophie. "Let's go."

We ran toward the pit while Paul – or the werewolf that used to be Paul – loped off toward the men. If they were smart, they'd be gone before he got there. Turned out they were plenty smart. They scattered and ran with Paul at their heels. He was showing a lot of self-control. He could have probably taken down all three of them and snapped their necks. Instead, he stayed a length or so behind them, herding them like a border collie. Norah and I crumbled the rest of the fruitcake we'd brought with us and waited.

It didn't take long. Within a few minutes, the first Kallikantzeroi poked its head up from the pit. "This way," I called. "Lots of fruitcake this way."

He snuffled the air and then began loping along the path we'd made, picking up chunks of cake and shoving them into his mouth. Another one followed him. And then it seemed like a flood of nasty-smelling, horned creatures were whipping their tails, shoving cake into their mouths all while heading toward Paul's van.

Just as abruptly, the flood went back to a trickle and then was over. "How many do you think that was?" I asked Sophie as I gathered up Paul's clothes. He'd want them later.

"No idea. I lost count at ten."

"I made it to twelve. I think less than twenty, though, right?" I wasn't sure how we'd keep more than twenty at the dojo for another eleven days.

"Sure," Sophie said, clearly thinking the same thing I was. "Less than twenty. Definitely."

Turned out there were twenty-four.

Paul met us at River City still in werewolf form. I'd grabbed his clothes from the construction site on our way to the van. I held them up and dropped them behind a hedge in the parking lot and returned to helping Sophie herd the Kallikantzeroi into the studio. In a matter of minutes, fully-clothed, mainly human Paul was back.

"So who were they?" I asked.

Paul shook his head. "They were mainly in pick-up trucks. A few SUVs. Nothing with a logo. I'm not sure it matters, at this point. Are they all in?" He pointed to the studio.

I nodded. "Let's go take a look."

Once we got in the door, I wished we hadn't. The scene was total chaos. Plus the smell was incredible, like a wall that I physically slammed into. "In the name of all that's holy, how do they stand themselves?"

Sophie leaned against the wall in the entryway. A row of colanders kept the Kallikantzeroi contained to the mat area. A few of them sat and counted holes in the colanders, muttering over and over to themselves, "one ... two ... one ... two."

Sophie shrugged. "You get used to it."

I stared at her. "Seriously?"

"Yeah. Plus we have bigger problems." She pointed out into the mat area.

Three Kallikantzeroi were using their taloned fingers to rip up shreds of the mats. "Why are they doing that?"

"They're bored. They don't have anything to do in here," Paul said in a muffled voice. He'd wrapped a bandana around the lower part of his face.

I turned to Norah. "Well, what do they like to do?"

"Rip apart holiday decorations, according to the grimoire," she said.

I sighed. "Let's go get us some trees."

Ted checked the Internet for which neighborhoods had green pick-up the following morning and we cruised through those, picking up discarded Christmas trees and wreaths and garlands. "Do you think we need to put ornaments on them?" I asked. "What if they don't want to rip apart bare trees?"

"No," he said firmly. "There are limits, Melina."

I wished he was right.

It was starting to get light by the time we were finished gathering up trees. Clara would be up and we weren't far from my parents' house. "Do you think we could swing by and pick her up on our way back to River City?" I asked.

Ted chuckled. "You miss her, don't you?"

I squirmed a little. "No. I just want to be considerate of my mother."

"Your mother loves taking care of her. Admit it. You miss your baby." He drove past the turn that would have taken us to my parents' house.

"You missed the turn." I looked over my shoulder and where we should have been.

"And I'll keep missing them until you admit it. You like being a mom."

He was right. I did like it. Everything about it had been unexpected from the pregnancy to the in utero zapping to the instant and immediate connection I'd felt to my daughter the second I first held her. She'd looked at me with those weird gray-blue newborn eyes and I'd been instantly shot through the heart.

"I miss Clara," I said.

He didn't say anything, but he did pull a Uey and head back toward my parents' house.

We pulled up in front of the karate studio armed with trees, coffee, and doughnuts. We'd left Norah, Alex, and Sophie on guard at the studio. Alex had already left – that whole rising sun thing really didn't agree with him – but Norah and Sophie were still there. "It's a good thing you finally got here," Norah said, grabbing a doughnut from the box and helping herself to coffee. "I'm not sure how much longer the building would stand. Those little suckers are destructive."

It must have really been bad for her to eat refined sugar and drink caffeine all at the same time. I peeked inside and almost howled. Mats had been ripped into shreds. Mirrors had been cracked. Ceiling tiles hung loose. "Let's get those trees in there."

I handed Clara to Norah. Ted, Sophie, and I started hauling in the trees and wreaths and lobbing them into the seething mass of Kallikantzeroi. The first few were ripped into dust before they could hit the ground. Once we'd lobbed them all in, I took Clara back from Norah and stood in the lobby watching the wild destruction.

One of the Kallikantzeroi ripped a branch off one of the trees and began running around in circles with it hooting.

Clara chuckled.

"You think that's funny, baby?" I asked. I loved her chuckles. They were so adorable.

Then she pointed her finger at the branch he was holding and the top of it burst into flame. She threw back her head and laughed. The Kallikantzeroi used that branch to light two more on fire. Clara laughed even harder. Her whole body shook. Ted grabbed the fire extinguisher off the wall and sprayed foam out into the room. The blaze went out. Clara looked at him with a frown and said, "Dadadadada."

Ted lifted the fire extinguisher. "I'll pick up a few more of these on the way home."

The next ten days were a blur of stealing discarded Christmas trees and wreaths, begging for fruitcake, and putting out fires Clara started. There were a few times where I honestly did not think I would make it, but then one miraculous morning I woke up and it was the sixth of January, Epiphany, the last surface day for the Kallikantzeroi. The world tree should have healed itself. They could go home without causing any kind of destruction.

I kissed its little square on the calendar. "I didn't think we'd see you, sweet Epiphany. I didn't think we'd make it."

"Anybody ever mention that you can be a little dramatic?" Ted came up behind me and wrapped his arms around my waist. "We've survived another crisis."

"Do you think they'll ever stop?" I asked.

"No." He turned me around to face him and kissed my forehead. "You don't want them to anyway. You'd get bored."

"I'd like to try it. Just to see, you know." I rested my forehead against his chest.

"Maybe when we're old." He chuckled.

"Sometimes I feel old now."

He picked me up by my waist and slid me onto the kitchen counter, pressing in close between my legs. He ran his hands up and down my arms. "Nope. Don't feel old to me."

Come to think of it, he didn't exactly feel old either. "Where's Clara?" I asked.

"Asleep."

I glanced over his shoulder at the clock. It was almost six-thirty. "Still? Do you think she's okay?"

He kissed me again. This time right on the lips. "I think we shouldn't question a good thing while we've got it. Hold on."

I wrapped my arms around his shoulders and locked my legs around his waist and he carried me back into the bedroom.

Clara slept until eight. I was almost frantic by the time she actually woke up. Frantic, but also relaxed and showered and dressed. Motherhood was so weird. "I wish we could take them back to the pit now," I said as I got her dressed.

"I know, but we have to wait until the site empties out. Luckily it gets dark early," Ted said.

I walked into the dojo with Clara on my hip and a bunch of Kallikantzeroi (a Kalliklatsch?) grabbed tree branches and lined up. Clara clapped and began pointing at them one by one, lighting them up like a row of Hanukkah candles. I sighed, set her down, picked up the fire extinguisher and put them all out. "You're a menace," I said, picking her back up.

"Mamamama," she said and kissed me.

Fine. She was my menace.

"We're down to about five fruitcakes," Sophie said, chewing on her lower lip. "Do you think it's enough?"

I tossed a bag to her. "I've got new supplies. Turns out Grandma Rosie and her friends are a great source for old fruitcake. They like it, but they're afraid they're going to lose teeth in those little fake fruits. I've got about fifteen more in here. Toss about ten to them. We need to save a few to lead them back to the pit."

"Good thinking."

It was a long day and the main way we survived was because we knew it was the last one. We'd gathered up as many discarded trees and decorations as we could find, but the Kallikantzeroi were still restless. Tumbling, rolling, begging Clara to set things on fire. I honestly thought I'd lose my mind a couple of times, but we made it to six o'clock. It was dark outside and the construction site should be deserted. Paul and Alex and Ted showed up and it was time to get our show on the road.

We crumbled up one of the remaining fruitcakes to lure the Kallikantzeroi out of the dojo and back into Paul's van. As back-up we had the route lined with colanders.

"Do you think we'll need to lure them back into the pit to go home?" Sophie asked. "Shouldn't their homing instinct or whatever they have be telling them that it's time to go back down now?"

I looked over at Paul. He shrugged and looked into the crowd of creatures. "Hey, Herb!" he called.

One of the creatures lifted a hand and waved. "Paul! How's it hanging, my man?"

"Can't complain. You guys ready to go home?"

Herb began jumping up and down excitedly. Paul turned back to me. "I'd say that's a yes."

"I still think we should save a loaf or two just in case." I took two of them and put them into my bag. "Okay, then. Let's go."

I opened the door to the dojo and Paul opened the back doors of the van. The Kallikantzeroi streamed along the fruitcake littered path, gobbling and shoving as they went. Paul slammed the back of the van shut after the last one hopped in. Sophie and I turned and shoulder to shoulder viewed what River City Karate and Judo had become.

"Oh, Melina," she sighed.

"Maybe I should let Clara loose on it. I'm not sure anything but fire could actually purify this." The floors were nothing but a tattered mess of fiber with scattered burn spots. The walls were streaked and filthy. Bits and pieces of ripped apart Christmas trees were scattered about. The whole place reeked. The smell was almost a visible fog on the floor.

"At the very least, we're going to need a lot of bleach," Sophie said.

We sighed and got in our cars to go to the construction site. I really didn't anticipate much trouble when we got there. The Kappas Construction people's plan had been to frighten the Kallikantzeroi into going home early and attacking the World Tree before it had fully healed. Too late for that now. It had had its full time to heal. There was no point in trying to keep them from going home, but we wanted to make sure they got there safely nonetheless.

We got to the site, Ted got out, popped Clara into her backpack, and took two fruitcakes from my bag. "I'll make a trail to the pit and text when I've got it set up."

I gave them both kisses and then watched them go on their way. Paul got out of his van and wiped his eyes on his shirt sleeve. "I'm going to have to have the van fumigated when this is done."

"Maybe we can get a package deal on your van and the dojo." I leaned against the side of the van and then immediately stood back up. I could smell them even outside the van.

"We'd probably still have to give them some kind of combat pay."

My phone buzzed. It was Ted down by the pit: Trail laid. Let 'em loose.

I signaled to Paul and he opened the van door. We watched as all twenty-four of our stinky little guests hopped out, saw the fruitcake trail, and took off for home. Paul whistled Follow the Yellow Brick Road.

"There's no place like home?" I asked. My phone buzzed again. It was Ted. Again. This time his message read: We've got company.

What kind of company? I texted back.

He texted: the kind that has a stack of chainsaws to give the Kallikantzeroi as they go home.

I showed Paul the text. "That'd bring the World Tree down a whole hell of a lot faster than a bunch of handsaws."

I texted back: on our way.

He texted: Clara holding them off for now, but hurry.

Clara? Holding them off? I didn't take the time to text back the question. Instead, I started running. Paul passed me before I was halfway to the pit. He got his shirt off, but his jeans basically disintegrated as he transformed while he ran. Alex was right behind him, gliding along close to the ground. Sophie and I glanced at each other and sprinted.

We got to the pit. Paul was on the far side from us of where the Kallikantzeroi were making their way back into the hole that led to their home. He was a beautiful wolf, thick at the shoulder and bristling with dark hair. His growl was so deep and strong, I could feel it in the pit of my stomach when we got close. He was holding off three men, each holding chain saws. Each time one of them tried to feint around him to get to the Kallikantzeroi, Paul lunged and snapped. Alex had two men busy in hand to hand combat. The Kallikantzeroi cowered in the near corner with one at a time making a break for it to get home.

I made it to where Ted stood. "How many of them have gone in?" I asked, gesturing at the Kallikantzeroi.

"Five," he said. We watched one more slip into the hole. "Six now."

Eighteen to go. Over by Paul, I heard the sound of a chainsaw starting. Werewolves, vampires, and Messengers heal fast, but not that fast. We turned to see one of the three men that Paul had been holding off had started his saw. Ted squeezed Clara's little leg. "Can you do it again, sweetie? Can you hit the man with the loud thing?"

Clara pointed a finger and sent a fireball toward the man with the chainsaw. It hit about three feet to the left of him, but it was enough to distract him for a moment. That was all Paul needed. He leapt and took the man down. The chainsaw went flying. The other two men dropped their saws and ran.

I turned not wanting to see the rest of the carnage, reaching up to turn Clara away, too.

"It's okay," Ted said. "He's not, well, you know …"

I did know. Or thought I knew. I turned back. Paul kept the man down using one huge paw. He snarled at the men who were fighting Alex. They, too, looked at their fallen comrade and ran. Paul lifted his paw and the man scrambled away.

"If he broke the skin anywhere," I said. Well, if he had, there'd be one more werewolf in the world.

Ted put his hand on mine. "Let's trust him to take care of it."

I nodded. I didn't see that I had another choice at the moment. "So that thing you did with Clara. Is that how you held them off before we got here?"

"Yep. Her aim is terrible, but shooting fireballs at men with chainsaws is kind of like horseshoes and hand grenades. Close counts." He craned his neck to look up at her. "Right, sweetie?"

"Dadadada," Clara said, clapping her hands.

Sophie jumped down into the pit to hurry the Kallikantzeroi back where they came from. It was a matter of minutes until the last one went home. Paul loped off and the rest of us trudged back toward our cars. "It's a good thing we have keys to his van," Ted said.

I grunted. One of these days, Paul was going to learn not to put his keys in his pants pockets if there was even the slightest possibility he was going to transform. Of course, none of us had thought we were going to be in the kind of situation where he'd have to change. I would never have brought Clara if I'd had the slightest idea, although it apparently was a good thing we had.

"You know what?" I asked Ted as we walked.

"No. What?"

"I am getting really tired of greedy 'Danes using 'Canes to do their dirty work."

He raised an eyebrow.

"That's always where I end up getting involved. It's neither Arcane nor Mundane so nobody pays attention, but all hell's breaking loose." I kicked at a loose rock. "That's what happened here. That's what always seems to happen. Then we all end up in danger trying to fix it."

"Not right now. Now we're safe," he said, looping an arm around my shoulder and pulling me close.

"I suppose," I said, snuggling in. "Not right now."

We ended up having to repaint the dojo to get the smell out. It had seeped into the walls somehow. On the other hand, Sophie and I had more help with our annual cleaning than we usually did. Paul and Ted both pitched in. We had too many windows for Alex to come by during the day and Norah had to work, but it went fast. We were on schedule to re-open by the eleventh of January.

I walked into my office to send out an email to the students. I went to sit down in my office chair and saw one last foil-wrapped loaf lying there. I shook my head. Sometimes these adventures seemed like a bad dream. Other times, I felt like I couldn't ever get away from them.

My stomach growled. It had been a few hours since breakfast. I unwrapped the loaf and broke off a piece.

"You know, this stuff isn't half bad." I broke off another piece and put it on the aluminum foil. I pulled Clara up onto my lap and pointed at the piece of fruitcake. "Toast that for Mommy, baby."

She clapped her hands and pointed.

ABOUT THE AUTHOR

Eileen Rendahl is the national-bestselling and award-winning author of the Messenger series and four Chick Lit novels. Her alter ego, Eileen Carr, writes romantic suspense. When she's not being one of the Eileens, she writes cozy mysteries as Kristi Abbott.

Both Eileens were born in Dayton, Ohio. She moved when she was four and only remembers that she was born across the street from Baskin-Robbins. Eileen remembers anything that has to do with ice cream. Or chocolate. Or champagne.

She has had many jobs and lived in many cities and feels unbelievably lucky to be where she is now and to be doing what she's doing.

Melina's adventures began in Don't Kill the Messenger and continue Dead on Delivery and Dead Letter Day. Don't miss Melina's previous holiday adventure in Dreidels and Demons or Payback for a Post-Mortem, a short story from the Messenger world.

Learn more about Eileen at www.EileenRendahl.com, like her on Facebook at www.facebook.com/EileenRendahlandEileenCarr or follow her on Twitter at @EileenRendahl. Or what the heck. Do all of the above!

HEART WIDE OPEN

ELIZABETH MAXWELL

Widow. It was a word that conjured up gray haired ladies in frumpy black dresses and veiled hats. It was not a word Julia Orchard associated with herself and yet she'd been wearing it for over two years now. The Widow Orchard. That poor girl. How does she manage?

The answer was she managed just fine. Or had until this particular December the twenty fourth when things suddenly went altogether sideways. Most people didn't schedule big meetings for the day of Christmas Eve but Julia was not most people and here she was zooming toward the forty second floor of 1166 Avenue of the Americas where she would convince the Beauty Now! executives and convince that if they hired her company, VonA Advertising, and followed her marketing plan, they would achieve skin care world domination. This in and of itself was not a problem. Julia had helped achieve world domination before, particularly in organic iced tea and thong underwear for athletes. Her reputation as a slayer of competing brands was practically legend, which was something considering she was barely twenty nine years old.

So needless to say, Julia was ready for the Beauty Now! people. She entered the large conference room on the forty second floor of 1166 Avenue of the Americas wearing four inch heels and a suit she considered her own personal Teflon. Nothing touched her in this suit. She was invincible and ready to offer her seemingly bottomless wisdom on how to sell youth to the sagging middle aged.

She smiled and greeted each executive seated at the narrow conference table by name. Each of them longed to be home wearing fuzzy slippers and wrapping presents, but this was Julia Orchard and she'd insisted. "You want to wait another day to kick Olay's ass," she'd said, "that's fine. But I wouldn't."

It was all going so well, just as she'd envisioned it! She could practically see the executives glowing as she described a recent investigative trip to CVS where she asked regular women, the kind with gentle laugh lines and crows feet, what they wanted from skin care. No, she couldn't give them back their twenties or make a failed relationship work but she could give them the light scent of lemon verbena and a firming lotion that might hold things up for the duration of the annual company holiday party.

"And this is what we're after with this marketing campaign," she told her enraptured audience. This was the part where she was to dazzle them with concept. Beauty Now! for a better You. In other words, you didn't have to look like a supermodel because even supermodels didn't look like supermodels. You just have to be yourself and that's plenty beautiful. Julia intended to use only real women in the ad campaign. Of course, she'd pick pretty ones but still, they wouldn't be ridiculous stick figures with lollypop heads. No human clothes hangers for Beauty Now!.

But Julia never got to the dazzle part because the door to the conference room opened and in walked Nick. Which was strange because Nick was dead.

CHAPTER 2

Naturally, everything went off the rails when Nick showed up. Julia froze, just like the champagne spewing ice statue at last week's drunken holiday party for the thong underwear company. Her mouth hung open. She blinked a few times. To those seated at the table, it appeared Julia Orchard was having a seizure of some sort but to point that out would be awkward so everyone just sat and watched.

After blinking failed to make Nick disappear, Julia began to sweat. It rolled down her back soaking the waistband of her Teflon suit pants. Why was it so damn hot in here? And why did the Executive Vice President of Sales wear so much perfume? What was she hiding? Julia pulled at the collar of her crisp white oxford. It was strangling her.

As the executives squirmed in their comfy leather chairs, Julia faced the floor-to-ceiling windows and tried to catch her breath. Outside was a panoramic view of New York City. A light snow was falling. She could see the Empire State Building. VonA's offices were downtown in a trendy loft district that had no view. It was the price of hipness.

When she turned back, she was sure the apparition would have disappeared but instead she found Nick wedged in next to the Executive Vice President of Product, a bony, angular woman whose Botoxed face carried a look of permanent surprise. Boy, she'd be surprised for real now.

"No!" Julia yelped. "Don't sit there!"

The EVP raised a professionally engineered eyebrow. "Excuse me?" she said. "Is everything okay?"

Of course not, Julia wanted to scream. The ghost of my dead husband is sitting on your lap! But she couldn't scream because her throat was closing, growing smaller and tighter and soon no air would pass through and she'd die right here on the floor of this fancy conference room while trying to sell moisturizer to the unsuspecting masses. There were many things in life that Julia didn't understand but there was something she knew for certain: she did not want to drop dead on the floor of this fancy conference room.

Sweat poured down her back. Her field of vision narrowed to nothing. "Excuse me," she gulped, grabbing the back of the perfumed EVP of Sales' chair for balance. "I think I need a minute." Despite everything, Julia managed to catch the look of pure horror on the woman's face as she fled the room.

By the time she got to the elevator banks, she would have chewed her own arm off if it meant a faster escape. People popped out of their cubicles to stare. A well-intentioned receptionist approached cautiously as if Julia might be rabid. Julia dodged hard left to avoid her. Her heart beat so quickly now she could see it thumping through her shirt.

Finally, the elevator arrived, blissfully empty, and Julia jumped aboard. She pushed her back against the wall and put her hands out to her sides for balance. She closed her eyes, panting and praying for an express trip to the ground floor.

But oh my god, what had she done? She'd run away from VonA's potentially biggest client this year! What would people think? What would her boss say?

"There you go again," came a voice. Julia's eyes flew open to find a wavy, transparent Nick standing before her in the elevator.

"Not real. Not real. Not real," she muttered, squeezing her eyes shut.

"But what is real, Julia? This elevator? Your favorite shoes? Isn't it all a construct?"

Well, that certainly sounded like Nick, casually philosophical in a way that ended conversations.

"I meant you weren't real," she said. "You're dead. I buried you. It wasn't that fun." Nick laughed at this and Julia could see right through his open mouth to the mirrored elevator wall behind him.

"Touché," he said. "But that doesn't change the facts. You just had a full on panic attack in front of a potential client and saw a ghost and what were you worried about? Your job, that's what. Success."

"That's not true!" she said.

"Don't kid yourself," Nick said. "You have this idea that you'll use real women in an ad campaign but it's not because you care about changing the ridiculous bar for what's considered beauty. You think it will create buzz. Right?"

"That's my job," Julia hissed.

"That's what the German soldiers said in World War II."

"Are you going there? Really? Wait. Don't answer that. Why am I having an argument with a figment of my imagination?" When were they going to reach the lobby? Out on the snowy street, in the freezing cold, surely this apparition would disappear?

"That's insulting," Nick said.

"I'm no longer addressing you because you don't exist."

"Fine. Be that way."

The elevator glided to a stop and the door opened on the festively decorated lobby. Julia smoothed invisible wrinkles from her pants and marched toward the exit. Out on the street, she continued on a pace, stepping gingerly over the homeless man blocking the corner.

Unfortunately, Nick continued on with her. "That man back there," he said. "Did you notice him?"

"Not real. Not real. Not real." Fortunately, on the streets of New York City, a woman could mutter to herself all day long and no one would pay her any mind.

"Of course you didn't notice him," Nick said, answering his own question. "You stepped over him. Do you know how many times you've done that? Do you know how many times other people have done that?"

It was cold out here and Julia had no coat, no gloves, no hat. She stuffed her fingers in her ears just like a child but somehow his voice stayed in her head.

"Too many people," he said, again answering his own question. "Let me tell you, Julia, I've changed. I see things very differently now."

Julia pulled up short and a pack of Russian tourists plowed right into her. "Of course you've changed," she shouted. "You're dead!"

"Hey lady!" one of the Russians yelled. "Look what you've done!" He'd spilled a steamy peppermint latte all over his expensive coat when they bumped and now assaulted her with a string of Russian expletives.

But this being a not so good day, she grabbed the rather large man by the lapels and yanked him close to her. "I don't care about your stupid drink," she hissed. "There's a moralizing ghost following me and I'm going to be fired."

The man held his hands up, signaling surrender. His friends backed away. When the Russians started to think you're crazy, well that wasn't good. Julia ducked into the subway mostly to escape. Her ears burned from the cold and her fingers were numb.

If up on the street was winter, down on the subway platform was tropical. All around her people sweated in their heavy parkas. The cold bits of Julia's body began to tingle as they warmed. She stomped her feet and rubbed her hands together, furtively glancing left and right. But the subway seemed to do the trick. Nick was nowhere to be found. Maybe ghosts don't appreciate extreme temperature fluctuations? In any case, she said to herself, it was probably the wine last night. Or the take out. Or her lack of sleep. Or lack of exercise. Or lack of interest in either.

Or maybe she was having a nervous breakdown? That was an interesting thought. Unfortunately, she'd left all her worldly possessions, including her cell phone, on the conference table at the Beauty Now! Headquarters so she couldn't quietly Google the symptoms that went along with losing one's mind.

As Julia squished onto a One train headed downtown, she caught a glimpse of her reflection in the grimy window. And staring back was a woman as ghostly as Nick.

CHAPTER 3

Back at her apartment in the East Village, things did not improve. Lady Di blocked the vestibule as usual. She liked to say she was the real Lady Di, having run away from the madness of Buckingham Palace to live incognito on the mean streets of New York City. But really she was a homeless lady of indeterminate age, who looked nothing like Princess Diana and who mostly just blocked the doorway.

"Excuse me," Julia said, climbing over her.

"The palace is so lovely this time of year," Lady Di mused from under a heap of dirty blankets. Her British accent was flawless. "I miss it. Perhaps I'll return?"

Julia didn't even bother to answer her. She slammed the door behind her and ran up the three flights of stairs to her apartment.

Inside, Nick was in his usual place on the expensive leather recliner but now Julia could see the pretty striped pillow right through his torso. This was jarring. Where were his internal organs? Or did being dead mean you no longer needed them and existed just as a shimmery outline of your former self?

These questions made her hands shake. Quickly, she uncorked a nice Pinot Noir and chugged it straight from the bottle. Little red rivers of wine ran down her chin but she didn't stop until half the wine was gone. A loud burb followed.

"Excuse me," she said wiping her face on the back of her white oxford shirt. Red wine stains didn't come out but who cared? She was being haunted.

"How sophisticated you've become in my absence," Nick said as she sat down on the couch, clutching her bottle.

"It's your fault," she said.

Julia Orchard had met Nick Hunt at a swanky New Years Eve party hosted by an investment banker friend who happened to have the most amazing Central Park West apartment. They found each other by the sushi spread and the rest, you might say, is history.

Friends were not surprised when they married the following year. Julia and Nick have a certain shallowness in common, they whispered. It's a very good match. It was true they liked the trendiest restaurants and thousand dollar shoes and vacations in St. Barts, but did that make them bad people? Not necessarily. They were perfectly happy attending charity balls as long as they weren't asked to work a soup kitchen on Thanksgiving. And so it went for two years. It's impossible to understand the inner workings of a marriage you aren't actually participating in, but friends tried anyway.

"They accessorize each other," was the way one person put it and that seemed accurate. Was there love or affection or desire or did they just look good together?

However, as time passed, this idea that they were somehow skin deep began to trouble Nick. He even went so far as to ask Julia if she really loved him.

"Of course I do," she'd said. "Why would you ask such a thing?"

He asked because he was experiencing a strange emptiness way down low in his belly, as if something were missing. In fact, he was standing on the corner of 34th and Broadway contemplating this emptiness when a cab jumped the curb and hit him. The doctors said death was instantaneous, that Nick didn't suffer. And so the Widow Orchard came to be.

Back on the couch, Julia chugged the wine, eyeing her companion. "What are you doing here?" she asked. Again, she was talking to a figment of her imagination but the wine made her feel better about it.

"You have to change your ways," Nick said.

"What are you, the ghost of Christmas Past?"

"Not hardly," he said. "But I've seen things. And I'm here to tell you things have to change."

"Change how?" she said. "I'm perfectly happy."

"Just look around," Nick said. "The world is in serious trouble." In the two years they were married the most serious topic broached was where to have Sunday brunch, followed closely by what they should wear to Sunday brunch. The world was for their pleasure. It was not something that required deliberate tending.

"And?"

"Every one person makes a difference," he said. "There's power in simple gestures of kindness. I see that now. I didn't see it before."

"How can you see anything?" Julia yelled. "You're dead!"

"Details," Nick said, waving her off. "It's too late for me, that's true." He waved a ghostly hand through the air as if to prove this point. "But not for you."

Julia didn't like where this conversation was going. The basis of their marriage had been fun. If it wasn't fun, they didn't do it. Why was Nick upset about that now?

After his death, Julia spent a full year mourning him. True, her mourning felt vague, as if she couldn't quite get her arms around it. This led to comments about how well she was managing. She looked pretty good for a young woman who had unexpectedly lost her husband and their potential future. But when the year of mourning ended, Julia got on with it. She had work to do and people to see and restaurant reservations. Life marched on.

In any case, Julia was beginning to suspect the second coming of Nick would not be brief. Her dead husband looked downright comfortable in his old chair even if he was see through. Julia started to laugh. This was awful. And tomorrow she'd probably get fired for literally running away from the Beauty Now! people. And she didn't even have her cell phone. How was a girl in modern society supposed to exist without a cell phone? It would be interesting to take a picture of Nick and see if he showed up. But maybe she was confusing ghosts and vampires? Would garlic scare away a ghost? Her laugh developed a slightly hysterical edge.

"What's funny?" Nick asked.

"I'm sitting here talking to you," she said. "That's pretty funny."

"I don't know why you'd think that," he said.

"Are you for real? Wait a minute. Don't answer that."

"You should eat something with that wine," Nick said.

"Don't give me advice," she said. "Please."

"Okay," he said. "But you need to sober up because we have things to do. And there's a time limit."

"What are you talking about?"

"Today is the twenty fourth of December. Christmas Eve," he said. "By Christmas morning, you need to have righted two wrongs."

"Are you kidding me with this?"

Nick looked grave, if a ghost could look that way. "I wish I was," he said quietly, "but no. I'm not kidding. Two wrongs corrected by sunrise Christmas morning."

There was something in his voice that gave Julia pause. While she very much wanted to leap from her seat and run out of the apartment, she remained. "Or?"

The shimmering glittery outline of a door appeared beside Nick. It seemed formed from a thousand Fourth of July sparklers. And although it was beautiful, beyond the door was a darkness deeper than any Julia had ever seen. And the darkness seemed to have form, something dense and alive. In short, it was terrifying.

"Come on," Nick said. "Time to go."

"In there?"

Nick nodded.

"No way. Forget it. I can't." But even as she resisted, her body floated toward the door and, screaming, she fell right through it.

Ass over teakettle, she plunged through the thick blackness. She wondered if this was what bungee jumping felt like and then she wondered why anyone would do such a thing on purpose? What the hell was going to happen when she landed?

"Nick?" she howled. "Where are you?" But her acceleration slowed and her feet came to rest on something solid.

In the distance was the shadowy outline of a house. As it drew closer, Julia saw a classic New England center hall colonial with candles in the windows and a wreath adorning the front door. The house twinkled with warm light and inviting energy. She felt herself smile even though she was mostly terrified. Through a pane of glass, she saw a towering Christmas tree bedazzled with white lights and red bulbs. Underneath the tree were dozens of elaborately wrapped gifts. It looked like a holiday card or a scene from a Lifetime Christmas special.

"Oh," she whispered, "it's so lovely."

There were people inside, too, dozens of them, all dressed in their winter best, smiling and talking. Children ran among them, dodging in and out of legs, laughing. There was champagne and clinking glasses and heartfelt wishes of Merry Christmas and Happy New Year. The smell of delicious food filled the air. Did she know these people? Yes. Some of the faces looked familiar even if she couldn't quite place them. Everyone in this neat package of a house was happy and just outside the window, Julia felt their happiness as if it were a thing she could reach out and hold. The sensation was sharp and bright and made her gasp.

Inside, the fireplace mantle overflowed with framed photos. Most of them were unclear but the one in the center was definitely the photo from her wedding day with Nick, the same one that still sat above the fake fireplace in her apartment. What was it doing here? There was a woman standing in front of the fire, a small blond child attached to her leg. She stroked the child's hair absently while she talked to someone. She smiled and laughed and abruptly, Julia realized she was staring at herself. She reeled back from the window.

"Nick! What the hell? Is that me?" Inside, a well dressed man approached the woman. He slipped an arm around her waist and kissed the top of her head. When he turned, she saw him full on. It was Nick.

"Oh my god," Julia whispered.

"Yeah," said Nick, appearing beside her. "So there's that."

"What does it mean?" she asked.

Nick shrugged. "A possible future," he said. "One of many."

"But you're...alive," she said.

"You're a quick study," he said. "Time to move on."

But Julia didn't want to move on. She wanted to drink up this moment. She wanted to roll around in it like a dog in the grass. A tug on her arm and she let go of the window ledge and fell backwards, once again bungee jumping in the dark without a rope. This time the landing was less smooth. She bounced a few times on a hard surface before coming to rest in a heap.

"Are you trying to kill me?" she shouted, disoriented from the fall.

"That was a little rougher than I expected," Nick said, floating down beside her. "Sorry."

"You've never done this before?" she said, crawling around on her hands and knees.

"Not exactly," he said. Before she could quiz him further on his qualifications for guiding her through these very vivid hallucinations, another image appeared in the distance, moving quickly toward her. But where she somehow knew the last image would be warm and welcoming, this one made the hair on the back of her neck stand on end.

"No," she said.

"Yes," Nick said. "You have to look, Julia. You must."

She tried to close her eyes but they refused. When the image arrived, she had no choice but to see it. There was nothing terrible on the surface. It was her apartment, a little rundown, a little dusty. There were Chinese take out containers on the coffee table and the low hum of the television in the background. And there she was, standing by the window, watching a light snow fall on the empty street below. She was older, with the same crows feet she'd seen on the women in CVS. Her mouth turned down at the corners as if frowning were it's natural resting position. Her whole body sagged, not from age exactly but from the weight of something greater.

On the mantle over the unlighted fireplace was the framed wedding photograph of her and Nick. It was Julia's favorite because while

Nick looked fine she looked amazing. It was a nice picture, which did not help explain why, in this scene, it filled her with dread. Here she was, middle aged, and the only photograph she had on her mantle was a wedding photo of her dead husband. There was nothing else.

The sting of regret, the thing that made her shoulders sag, hit her hard in the chest. There was so much emptiness, a bottomless loneliness that devoured everything in its path. Julia stumbled backwards. She reached to hang on but there was nothing to grab. She was falling again.

CHAPTER 4

"Oh my God!" Julia awoke on the couch with a start. She hadn't moved an inch but her heart raced as if she'd just crossed the finish line at the New York Marathon. The clock on the wall indicated two minutes had passed. "What the hell just happened? What was that?"

"Potential futures," Nick said from his comfy chair. "Like I said." He appeared to be examining his cuticles even though he didn't actually have cuticles.

Julia stood abruptly, forgetting about the wine bottle clenched between her thighs. The bottle flew into the air and landed on the white shag carpet bought just last year. The carpet was perfect, so retro hip that when she first rolled it out, it filled her with happiness. But it was not the happiness that wrapped around her at the house filled with Christmas revelers. No. That was something different. A blood red stain spread slowly across the carpet.

"Bummer," said Nick. "Although I never would have gone with shag in here personally."

Julia left the bottle where it fell. "What are the two things?" she asked quietly.

"I thought you'd never ask," he said with a ghostly grin. "But here's the trick. You have to think of them yourself. That's part of the deal."

"But how?" Julia yelped. "What if I don't choose the right wrongs?"

"Oh damn."

"What?"

"I forgot to read you the fine print," he said. "I'm supposed to do that at the beginning, like Miranda rights but, you know, more of disclaimer in this case."

"What on earth are you talking about?"

"So you right two wrongs but if they're not the correct wrongs as determined by forces beyond your ability to understand in your present state and so one and so forth, you still might end up an old lady in out of fashion clothes, all alone in this dusty apartment with no one who loves you or who you love."

"I don't like this deal," Julia said. "This sounds like a lousy deal."

"This is a leap of the most profound kind, Julia. A leap of faith. Do you believe your choices have power, even the minor ones?"

Julia leaned back on the couch. She felt dizzy and nauseous. How did it come to this? How did she end up here bargaining for her future with a dead man?

"For the record," she said, "this sucks."

Nick sighed and if she closed her eyes, it almost felt like he was alive. A sharp ache stabbed her in the chest. Now that he was here, sort of here anyway, she missed him.

"Tell me about it," he said. "Now, we don't have much time. When the sun comes up on Christmas morning, you need to be done."

"You said that already."

"Did I?" Nick leaped to his feet. It was a surprisingly silent move. "So what are we waiting for? What are your two wrongs?"

Did he smirk because when it came to wrongs Julia had a long and distinguished list from which to pick? She did not like to think of herself this way. It was very uncomfortable.

"I don't know," she said. "I don't even know where to start."

"Back when I was alive," Nick said, "I always felt like a walk helped when I was stuck with something. I'd walk around in Central Park until I figured out my problem. Did you know that about me?"

Julia shook her head.

"I even invited you once to join me but you said no. Something to do with thong underwear, I think?"

For some reason, the idea that she'd turned down her husband's request for a walk in the park brought tears to her eyes. "I'm sorry," she muttered.

"I'm not trying to make you feel bad," Nick said, "but let's take a walk."

On the way out, Nick greeted Lady Di. "Good evening, your Highness," he said.

"Good evening, kind Sir," Lady Di responded, peeking out from under her blankets.

"Wait! You can see him?"

Lady Di gave her a dirty look. "I'm homeless," she said, "not blind."

"Come on, Julia," Nick said. "Let's roll."

Fifteen minutes later Julia strolled up a nearly empty Park Avenue, the snow falling harder now, the ghost of her dead husband whistling Jingle Bells at her side. Ten blocks later, they turned west on 23rd Street. Half way down the street, they stopped in front of a dingy brick three story building. The lower level was a bodega, open despite the holiday. Snow covered the display of brightly colored apples. Inside, an old man in an apron shuffled around with a feather duster, cleaning cans of beans and soup. The second story was dark but lights were on up on the top level.

"I think I know why we're here," Julia whispered.

"I thought you might," said Nick.

CHAPTER 5

Mac McKinley was six months into his big entrepreneurial experiment, the McKinley Agency. He'd finally worked up the nerve to escape the big soul sucking advertising agency and start his own shop. He left with dreams of monster success and never once thought it might not happen. It was the American dream after all and why not him?

But things had not been going smoothly. He'd landed just five clients, all of which collectively did not pay enough to keep the lights on in the tiny offices on 23rd Street. He'd poured his life savings into this venture and was on the verge of despair when, just that morning, he'd been selected to present a concept to the internationally renowned toy making company, Building Bricks, which was releasing a line for girls. He was so excited by this prospect that when a twenty two year old Julia Orchard wandered in off the street to pass a resume to his nonexistent receptionist, he'd hired her on the spot. He liked her old school initiative, pounding the pavement, so to speak. Plus, he couldn't show up to a pitch meeting for a company like Building Bricks alone. He needed gender balance! He needed warm bodies! It helped that Julia was gorgeous in that effortless way young people have.

On her first day, Mac discovered Julia had a degree in English Literature from a small up state liberal arts college, which meant she could talk the hell out of Shakespeare but didn't know how to do much else. However, she was eager to learn and for the next six weeks, they set about creating a campaign for Building Bricks that felt fresh and lively. They stuck to primary colors, avoiding the pink trap. They leaned heavily on engineering concepts and shouted the word "Princess!" at each other whenever they veered off into terrain considered much too girly. Fueled by caffeine, they worked night and day, occasionally dashing home for a shower and change of clothes. Mac fantasized about what it would be like to land Building Bricks as a client. He could hire more staff and move to bigger offices. He could shamelessly name drop at all the cocktail parties he'd inevitably attend. He could eat something other than rice and beans at every meal.

He fantasized about Julia, too. They were so in tune with one another. He'd never met a woman who got him quite the way Julia did. Sure, he was a solid decade older than she was and she worked for him. But still, when she was leaning over his desk, spilling out of her lacy pushup bra, he could barely breathe. He could see himself falling in love with her.

The day of the pitch arrived. Mac met Julia on the sidewalk outside the Building Bricks headquarters on Broadway. The glass building reflected the morning sun and, despite the bags under his eyes, Mac felt suddenly exhilarated. This was it! This was his moment! Even the lobby smelled of success.

The pitch was perfect. Julia had them eating out of the palm of her hand, flipping her blond hair and grinning with youthful energy. They clearly loved her so Mac let her take the lead and run with it, pride swelling his chest By the end of the meeting, the Vice President of Marketing shook their hands with great enthusiasm and said he'd be in touch.

They celebrated with hot dogs from a vendor in Central Park. They replayed how awesome they were over and over. They moved on to a bar and drank cheap beer, giddy with success. That night they fell into Mac's unmade bed and he finally got to remove that silky push up bra and run his hands over those creamy perfect breasts. It was all coming together. The next morning he left Julia sleeping and slipped out for coffee and bagels. When he returned, she was gone.

She didn't answer her cell phone. She didn't answer the buzzer at her apartment. And she didn't come to work. For three days, he heard from neither Julia nor Building Bricks. On the fourth day he finally got the Vice President of Marketing on the phone.

"Mr. McKinley," the man roared. "So good to hear from you!"

"I thought I'd check on whether you'd made your decision about the new campaign," he said with more confidence than he felt. The world was sand beneath his feet.

"Yes, yes, of course. You were on my list to follow up with today." The man cleared his throat and Mac knew what was coming. They were going in 'a different direction. "We've decided to go in a different direction."

"But why?" Mac blurted. "I thought we had great synergy in that room together." Had he really just used the word synergy? Things were bad. Very bad.

There was an uncomfortable pause. "Have you spoken to Ms. Orchard recently?"

Why was he asking about Julia? "No," Mac said.

"Well, she said she'd be in touch with you but maybe you missed each other." Again, he cleared his throat. "We very much liked Ms. Orchard's ideas and enthusiasm for this project. Being a young woman, she brings a certain something to the table. But..."

"But?"

"We're a billion dollar company, Mr. McKinley," he said, "so let me be frank. Your shop is just too small."

"We can scale!" Mac yelled, despite all attempts to stay calm. "We can bring in more bodies, whatever it takes!"

"Time is of the essence here, you understand, so we asked if Ms. Orchard would be amenable to, ah, joining VonA Advertising."

Had he just said VonA Advertising? "Excuse me?"

"VonA Advertising? Surely you've heard of them?"

Of course, he knew VonA! They'd stolen his last ten years! They'd taken his ideas and never given him credit for any of them! VonA was the reason he was out on his own. He could not believe he was hearing this.

"So you stole my employee and gave the business to my competitor?" Mac said finally.

"Oh, it wasn't my idea," the Vice President of Marketing laughed. "It was Julia's! And she said she wasn't your employee, just helping out on this campaign as a favor. Clever young woman. She's going places. Don't you agree?"

Mac was speechless. This had to be a joke. Without another word, he hung up the phone, put on his jacket and stormed out into the bright sunshine. He paced in front of Julia's building for three hours until she finally showed up, a VonA tote bag slung over her shoulder. The thing that got Mac, killed him, was her casual smile as if everything was right with the world. Which, he imagined, it was. If you were Julia Orchard and not Mac McKinley.

He'd come for a confrontation, to yell and scream and howl but the moment he saw her dirty little smile and that goddamn tote bag, he just deflated, the emotion required for pitching a fit much too great. He was limp with betrayal.

"Mac!" she said when she saw him, slumped against her building. "How are you?" Her wide eyes brimmed with concern. She was a superb actress! She might be the best he'd ever seen! "I tried to call you." When she reached out to touch him on the shoulder, he recoiled.

"You didn't," he said. "Please don't lie."

"I did," she said. "I promise. I had fun the other night."

The girl had no shame. Not only did she play him, she stole his potentially career making client right out from under him. "You're a bad person," he muttered.

"Pardon?"

"I said you're a bad person. No good. Rotten. How could you?"

"Well," she said curtly, "I have to take care of myself. I saw an opportunity and I took it. You'd have done the same."

But she was wrong. Mac McKinley was made of different stuff. He should have been a doctor or a firefighter. His soul did not allow for the casual destruction of other people's lives. He shook his head sadly.

"I'd like to think karma will some day come back and bite you on the ass," he said. "But people like you, you take and take and keep on taking and never seem to pay the price."

Julia shrugged but there was a flicker in her eye that suggested maybe she ought to heed what this man was saying. She didn't, of course, and as soon as Mac walked away, she promptly forgot all about him.

Until now.

CHAPTER 6

"I didn't mean to hurt him," Julia said, staring up at the lighted top floor windows in the grungy building.

"He kept on with the business, despite your betrayal." The matter-of-fact way Nick put this made Julia wince. She'd never thought of it as betrayal. She'd considered it a career move and if you were going to succeed in this town, a certain level of brutality was required and accepted "But he never got a chance with a company like Building Bricks again."

Nick strode toward the door and it yielded without a touch.

"Where are we going?" Julia asked.

"Inside. Upstairs."

"Why?"

"To right the wrong."

"I don't know how to do that," she whispered. That she'd have to look Mac McKinley in the eye was far scarier than being haunted. "What do I say?"

Nick paused, an exasperated expression clouding his transparent face. "That's not something I can help you with," he said. "What do you feel?"

"Sick to my stomach? Filled with dread?"

"You're hopeless. Come on."

Reluctantly, Julia followed Nick into the building and up the narrow stairs to the third floor landing. Her throat was dry, her hands clammy. Through the glass pane in the office door, she saw everything was much the same as it had been seven years ago. Mac sat with his feet up on the single desk, leaned way back in his chair, eyes closed. It was Christmas Eve. What was he doing here?

Standing in the hallway peering in on Mac, Julia was filled with a strange tingling sensation as if an electrical current was coursing through her veins. All her senses heightened in an uncomfortable way. She shivered.

"Go on," Nick urged. Where was he now? The man had an infuriating way of flickering in and out of her reality. She took a small step toward the door and then another. Mac's eyes flew open at the gentle knocking.

At first he squinted. Julia could see him running through all the plausible explanations for her presence outside his office door. He was dreaming. He was hallucinating. It wasn't actually her, just her very lost clone. Someone slipped something into his rice and beans. Before he could say otherwise, Julia pushed open the door and invited herself in.

The office smelled like stale coffee and desperate sweat and she crinkled up her nose. Around Mac's eyes were deep wrinkles and his face seemed to sag around the chin. His hair was thinner than she remembered and gray around the temples. He wore a tie, loose at the neck with his sleeves rolled up to his elbows. His hands were chapped and red as if he'd never heard of gloves. She gave him a little wave.

"Mac," she said.

"Julia Orchard," he said. "Julia Fucking Orchard. Am I actually asleep or is this some kind of nightmare?"

"Neither," Julia said. She tried to smile but her lips felt rubbery. "It's karma, I guess. I wanted to say I'm sorry."

Mac leaped up, overturning his desk chair with such force Julia flinched. "You're sorry?" he hollered. "Seven years and you're sorry?"

She nodded, eyes cast down. The tingling grew more intense. Her skin jumped and quivered. And in the pit of her stomach, she knew what Mac had felt that day, the last time she'd seen him out in front of her apartment. It was happening to her. It was happening right now! It was a potent mixture of betrayal and anger and self doubt, of longing and fear and anxiety. And it was all because of her.

"Oh!" she gasped, wobbling on her feet. Mac's eyes filled with concern. Even now, even after all she'd done to him, he didn't relish her pain.

"I don't….know what to say," she said. "I know sorry isn't enough. It's nothing. I didn't know! I didn't understand. But now I do. I think I do. Mac, I'm so sorry."

"You ruined everything," he said simply.

Tears pricked her eyes. When was the last time she'd cried? She couldn't actually remember. People assumed she did all her crying in private after Nick died. They called her strong. But the truth was she'd never cried over Nick. Not one single tear. But now they streamed down her cheeks.

"Hey," Mac said, coming around from behind the desk. "Stop that. It was a long time ago. I'm over it."

But she shook her head. He was lying. He'd never gotten over it. He still carried around a thimble full of humiliation, deep down in his belly. It colored things in his life.

"I'll make it up to you," she said.

"There's nothing to make up," he said.

"Oh but there is!" The tingling was so intense now she could barely stand. "Nick!" Where the hell was that dead husband of hers when she needed him?

Just beside Mac, the shimmering door appeared. Not this again. Slowly, it sucked her forward, leaving her feeling vague, fluid almost, as she passed right through. This time she didn't scream.

On the other side, she was young. Not that twenty nine was old exactly but this was Julia at twenty two. From her perch just outside the scene, Julia watched the younger version of herself cruise down 23rd Street in the blazing summer sun. The city smelled like garbage baking in an oven. Had she really worn those white pants and red shoes? What was she thinking?

"Now, now," said Nick, quavering beside her.

"What am I doing here?" she demanded. "Why am I watching myself? How does this right a wrong? I told Mac I was sorry."

"Yes you did," said Nick. "And I mostly believe you meant it. Which is a vast improvement already. But to right a wrong something has to change. Keep watching. You'll see what I mean."

It was weird to watch herself. Overall, the experience made her twitchy and uncomfortable. There she was, a bundle of fresh resumes tucked under her arm, practically skipping down the sidewalk. When she arrived at the address for the newly minted McKinley Agency, she stopped abruptly, a frown appearing on her flawless face. She stared for a long moment at the windows on the third floor, shielding her eyes from the sun.

Julia whispered to her young self, "Don't go up. Please. I don't trust you. I know what you'll do."

For a moment, young Julia appeared to move toward the building's door but she stopped just short of pulling it open. She froze, spinning around as if grabbed from behind. But there was no one, just the old guy from the bodega, whistling a tune and putting peaches on display in neat rows.

"Hello miss," he said.

"Hello," young Julia said.

"Peach?" Without waiting for a yes, the old man threw a ripe piece of fruit to Julia who reached up and caught it. It was a perfect peach. "Go on," the man urged.

So she did. She sunk her teeth into its ripe fresh, the juice running down her chin. And she kept right on walking down 23rd Street, eating her peach, away from Mac McKinley.

But now the scene changed again. The past was gone. She was back on the present side of the shimmering door from hell. But it didn't look like the McKinley Agency she'd been in moments ago. No, this office was big and modern and packed with people, drinking and eating dim sum. This was a party. And there in the middle of a throng of people was Mac. He stood tall, grinning ear to ear. He slapped people on the back. He handed out little presents. There was love in the room. There was camaraderie.

"Where the hell am I?" Julia said. "Nick! Nick?"

"Excuse me, but do we know each other?" It was Mac, right in front of her, eyes curious. God, he was gorgeous! How come she never noticed that before? "Because I feel like I know you."

"No," Julia stammered. "We...I....I think I walked into the wrong party. I'm so sorry."

"Well, you can stay," he said smiling. "Maybe this is fate?"

"I'm sorry," she said slowly, "but I'm due at another affair. Merry Christmas." And before he could ask her name, she slipped out of the office and disappeared.

CHAPTER 7

Julia ran from the building like Cinderella at 11:59. Outside on the sidewalk, she stopped to catch her breath. She was on Madison Avenue at 51st Street, a long way from the dumpy offices on 23rd. This weird time travel geography bending produced a unique sort of motion sickness and she tucked her head down as if on a plane doomed to crash.

"It does take some getting used to," Nick said.

"I'm going to puke."

"Please don't."

"What was that, Nick?" When she looked up, he was wavier than before. But was it her or him?

"There's great power in small acts of kindness," Nick said.

"But all I did was walk by his office," she said. "I didn't do anything! I did the opposite of something. I did nothing."

"Sometimes the best thing you can do for a person is let them go," Nick said.

"You sound like a Hallmark card," she said. "A bad one. The ones they sell for ninety nine cents because they don't make any sense."

"A small act," Nick sighed. "Great impact. See?"

"No," she said, "I don't see. I really think I'm going to throw up."

Nick glanced at his watch, a heavy expensive thing that seemed to float on his transparent wrist. "We don't have time for that right now. We have to move if we're going to get this next wrong righted in time."

The night felt thick and syrupy as Julia reluctantly followed Nick down the empty sidewalk. She had no idea what time it was. Were people at home with loved ones wrapping presents and drinking champagne and telling children that Santa wouldn't come unless they went to bed? Or was it later than that? Was everyone asleep, visions of sugar plums already dancing in their collective heads?

"Where are we going?" she asked, scurrying to catch up with Nick. He glided over the snow, leaving no footprints, whereas her shoes were soaked through. And they were tennis shoes! Scuffed ones at that. She didn't even own tennis shoes! Something was definitely happening.

"We're going back to school," Nick said.

"Can you please be a little more specific?"

"Not really."

"God, are all you ghosts so obtuse?"

"I don't know. I don't know any ghosts."

"See what I mean?"

"You should pick up the pace," Nick said. "Remember what I said about time?"

"Of course I do," Julia shouted. "I'm going to turn into a sad pathetic lonely old cat lady unless we get this done by sun up!"

"No cats."

"What?"

"Cats are special. You won't have any."

She trudged on through the snow, muttering nasty things at Nick that he pretended not to hear. They passed a young couple, cheeks red with the cold. They held hands, eyes only for each other, laughing and stopping to kiss every few feet. A strange icy fist wrapped around Julia's heart. These two people, they were in love. Real love. 'Lie down in front of a train for you' love. 'Go to the ends of the earth looking for you' love. 'You had me at hello' love. A love Julia had never experienced. If she'd been asked to throw herself in front of the car that killed Nick, saving him and sacrificing herself, her answer would have been an emphatic 'no'. The world existed in relation to her. She was at its center. She knew no other way of being.

But for these two, the world was an enormous tapestry where they could write the story of their love. It would go on and on, into all the tiny nooks and crannies, places they could only imagine now. They would make it better simply because they wanted it to be better for each other.

As they passed on the sidewalk, a tendril of their emotion reached out and tickled her. It was intoxicating, a combination of the best wine and chocolate and the sun warming your face and your toes in the sand. It was the reason for everything and as the couple moved away, a deep loss squeezed her tight.

"Nick!" He was quite a ways ahead now. She could barely see him in the shadowy streetlights. "Wait!" When she caught up to him she tried to grab his arm but her hand went right through him.

"Do you know why I'm like this?" she demanded.

"Like what?"

"Like this! Why can't I be like those two?" She pointed at the couple disappearing in the snow. "Why can't I feel that?"

"You can," Nick said simply. "But you're lazy. Your choices are the easy ones. You never want to be inconvenienced or put yourself out there for anyone. There's very little risk in the way you live. And very little reward."

Had Nick called her self centered and shallow during their marriage, she would have been offended. She would have gone out and done some retail therapy, probably returning home hours later with three or four pairs of shoes and a puffy face from one of Anika's Supremely Expensive Facials.

But now she considered what he was saying, and after doing that for a moment she realized he was mostly right. It's not that she was actively disdainful of other people and their problems but she just didn't notice them. Unless they had a direct influence on her, they might as well not exist. She knew people who picked up trash in Central Park, collected winter coats for the homeless, who delivered Meals on Wheels to the elderly on the weekend. She knew people who donated their hair to cancer patients and sent soccer balls to Mali. She even knew people who gave to public radio every time they asked. But the pressure of the world's many needs never pushed hard enough on the hard shell of Julia Orchard to motivate her to action.

Suddenly, Julia had the sense she might be terribly wrong about all this and her chest grew tight. But when she tried to explain to Nick, he waved her off.

"I'm sure the personal insights upon which you stumble this evening are fascinating," he said, "but we're in a bit of a rush. Let's go!"

She had to run to keep up with him. It never occurred to her how strange she must look running down the sidewalk in the snow, talking to herself. And it looked pretty strange indeed.

They were on the Upper West Side now, on Columbus Avenue. They passed the Museum of Natural History, covered in snow. Two blocks later, they stopped at the 24-hour Happy Chinese Diner. Inside, Julia could see just two customers hunched over cups of coffee she bet had long gone cold. A waitress sat at the wide Formica counter, chewing on a pencil, a folded newspaper in hand. There was something familiar about the woman but Julia couldn't place it. The bell above the door tinkled merrily as Nick held it open.

"In we go," he said.

"I thought we were in a rush," Julia asked. "Why are we stopping for food? You don't actually eat, do you?"

"Of course not," he said, annoyed. "Ghosts don't eat. But we're not here for the fortune cookies."

At the sound of the door opening, the waitress heaved her bulk off the bar stool and shuffled her way toward the new customers, although she could see only one.

"How are you doing tonight?" she asked, pulling a menu off a pile by the door. "Pretty outside, isn't it?" Finally she looked at Julia, really looked at her. The menu in her hand fluttered to the ground.

"You," the waitress said simply. "It's you."

Julia squinted at the nametag on the woman's red and white uniform. "Gaby" it read. "Gabrielle Hudson," Julia said. And now it made sense why she was here even if she wished very much that it didn't.

CHAPTER 8

By seventh grade the students at The Smith School for Girls, tucked away on Manhattan's Upper West Side, had known each other forever. Most of them had been together since kindergarten and while occasionally a girl left or a new one came, things remained pretty constant. After seventh grade, the last year they could attend Smith, the girls would scatter throughout the city to private schools of varying flavors.

To say these girls were privileged was an understatement and to an outsider their sense of entitlement verged on distasteful. But they were twelve and thirteen. They didn't care about coming across as arrogant. In fact, most of the girls modeled this behavior on arrogant parents, who saw absolutely nothing wrong with raising insufferable little brats. Julia Orchard was one of them.

Gabrielle Hudson was not. Sure, she attended The Smith School for Girls, but that was where the similarities ended. Gabrielle was a scholarship student. The Smith School, for strictly PR reasons, offered a single student per grade a full ride each year. When you did the math that meant there were just seven such students in the entire school of over five hundred girls. It would have been eight if the Smith board had not decided against offering such a spot in kindergarten. They came to the consensus that doing so was beyond the call of duty and much more generous than they could be expected to be. Gabrielle had gotten the spot because the girl who had originally been part of this class up and moved to Florida.

Gabrielle lived in Washington Heights before Washington Heights was cool. She lived there when it was gritty and a little dangerous. She shared a one bedroom apartment with her mother and younger brother, both of whom were smarter again by half than the majority of the Smith students and their parents. Gabrielle's mother was a librarian so this meant they had no money but the house was full of books and both children read voraciously. When an opportunity came for Gabrielle to fill the vacant spot at The Smith School, it took her mother less than a second to decide.

Yes, Gabrielle would join the girls at Smith. This was a fateful decision in many ways. For one, it put Gabrielle on the path that eventually led to The 24-hour Happy Chinese Diner on the Christmas Eve shift. But for now, she was on The Smith School seventh grade field trip to the Museum of Natural History. They'd walked from school, in two neat rows much like the little girls in the Madeleine books. Every girl had a partner except for Gaby, who lingered at the back of the line. Field trips were the worst because there were so many opportunities for the mean girls to get at her out of sight of the teachers.

They were in the Milstein Family Hall of Ocean Life, the one with the ninety four foot long model of the blue whale dangling from the ceiling. The tour guide, an elderly man clearly delighted by the whale, went on and on. Julia stood near her friend Charlotte who stood next to Annalisa who was behind Gaby.

"An adult blue whale," the tour guide intoned, "weighs roughly 420,000 pounds. Can you imagine something that large that's alive?"

"Yup," whispered Annalisa. And she poked Gaby in the back. Charlotte giggled. Gaby winced but didn't turn around.

"Blue whale in a Smith uniform," Charlotte said. "Who knew they came in size ginormous?"

Charlotte and Annalisa looked to Julia. It was her turn to insult Gaby. It wasn't that Julia had anything against Gaby exactly but she was part of a tribe that demanded she do her part. If she didn't, she'd be next on the hit parade. That's how these things worked.

"You really are fat," Julia said to Gaby. "And you have a stain on your uniform shirt."

This was the moment the tour guide hustled them away to see the squid exhibit but Gaby froze in place. It wasn't like these girls hadn't been mean to her before but there was something in Julia's expression, a smug disgust, that just about brought Gaby to her knees. She would never be good enough. She could go to Harvard and get elected President of the United States and she still wouldn't be good enough.

Her vision narrowed and she felt dizzy. She was the big fat slob of a scholarship student who lived in a shitty apartment in Washington Heights and she would never have any friends. No one would ever love her because why would they? There was a loud ringing in her ears and in the moment before she passed out, she heard Jennifer say, "Check it out, the whale looks like she's going to faint."

"It'll be a tsunami," Charlotte added with a giggle.

CHAPTER 9

Gaby narrowed her gaze on Julia. "What are you doing here?" she asked.

"I want to say," Julia began, "well, I want to say I'm sorry for being so...mean." Her skin jumped and quivered just like it did before with Mac McKinley. And she was right there with Gaby under the blue whale. The humiliation and shame filled all her cells. She could barely breathe. "I'm just...I know it can't mean anything now but I'm so sorry."

Gaby gave a sharp laugh. "Look at you," she said, "feeling bad now, are you? Is that it? Are you a twelve stepper? Because that Charlotte came by a few months ago to apologize. Said the program required she make amends. She didn't look sorry though. She just looked hung over."

"I'm not in the program," Julia said quietly. "I just want to make this right. How do I do that? How do I make it right?"

"Oh that's rich," Gaby said. She stalked off toward the diner's counter and slid behind it. "But I'll be honest with you, I'm not sure how to answer that."

"We hurt you," Julia said flatly.

"You derailed me," Gaby hissed. "You made me think I was worthless and I've struggled every day to convince myself you weren't right. Why did you do that? Did it make you feel good?"

"No," Julia said. "No. I don't know why we did it. We were just... mean."

"Well, thanks for coming by but you can't fix the past so you might as well leave. Okay? Just leave. I don't want you here."

The tingling was intense now. The shimmering door appeared beside Gaby.

"Oh no," Julia muttered. "I hate this part."

"What?" Gaby demanded.

"Nothing," Julia said. "Just…I'll see you in a bit."

It was as if all Julia's molecules disassembled as she was dragged through the door. Coming back together was harsh but here she was, right under that damned blue whale, with a clear view of her twelve year old self. The tour guide had just laid out the fact that the blue whale's penis is ten feet long, leaving the girls in fits of giggles. Young Julia laughed so hard she stumbled into Charlotte.

"Hey!"

"Sorry," Julia said quietly.

"What's wrong with you?" Annalisa whispered, eyes like daggers.

What had Julia ever seen in these girls? Why did she so desperately need them to like her?

"Nothing," Julia shot back. "I tripped. Jeez."

"Whatever."

From back here Julia could see Gaby, her hair done in neat corn-rows. She tugged on the skirt of her ill fitting uniform. Julia's heart lurched. What pleasure was there to be had in tormenting this person?

"An adult blue whale weighs 420,000 pounds," the tour guide said. "Can you imagine something that large that's alive?"

Here it comes, thought grown up Julia. This is the moment.

"Yup," said Annalisa, reaching out to poke Gaby in the back. Fast as lightening, young Julia dropped her backpack on Annalisa's foot.

"Ow!" Annalisa yelped.

"Oh my god," Julia said, eyes wide in mock horror. "I'm so sorry. I was just really distracted by the ten foot penis idea."

Charlotte giggled and moments later the three girls were banished to the back of the pack for laughing out of turn. But Annalisa never poked Gaby. And Charlotte never called her a whale. And Julia never told her she was fat and sloppy.

This time the change of scene was so abrupt, and the motion sickness so extreme, that Julia found herself crouched down next to an elegant brownstone somewhere in upper Manhattan retching in the fresh snow. An elegantly wrapped fruitcake sat in the snow before her.

"Oh god," she said. "This has to stop."

"You look like shit," Nick said.

"Well, at least I'm alive," Julia shot back. "Sort of."

Nick shrugged. "I guess you have a point. How was that?"

"I don't know," she said. "Awful? I can't tell if I did the right thing because I knew it was the right thing to do or if I really just dropped my backpack and derailed events by accident? What's with the fruitcake?"

"We should have a look inside," he said, climbing the steps of the brownstone. Through the large bay windows, Julia saw a woman on a couch, beside a small Christmas tree. She held a baby in her arms, singing and swaying like new moms do. Julia could hear inside the room perfectly even though she was out on the steps.

"This is weird," she said to Nick.

"I'd think by now you'd be over saying that," he said.

"Never," she said.

The baby slept quietly in the blankets. The woman swayed and rocked. A man entered the room, tall and good-looking. He carried a tray with steaming coffee mugs and a plate of Christmas cookies.

"Hey darling," he said. "You need me to take over?"

"No," said the woman. "I'm good. Maybe just keep me company for a few minutes?"

"Nothing I'd like to do more than hang out with my favorite girls. You look beautiful." The man slid in beside her on the couch.

The woman laughed, a familiar sound, but deeper and more robust than Julia remembered it. Gaby. "I haven't had a shower in two days. I'm due back at the firm after New Year's and I have no idea how I'm going to pull that off." But even as she said it, she smiled. She was happy.

The man wrapped his arms around Gaby and the baby. "You will," he said. "You'll know. That's who you are."

"Thank you," she said, pulling the man in close for a kiss. He slid a hand up her sweater and she sighed with pleasure. It would have gone further had a knock at the front door interrupted.

It was Julia knocking, fruitcake in hand. What the hell? She glanced around frantically for Nick but he was nowhere to be seen. The door swung open and there was Gaby, her gorgeous husband and her bundle of newborn joy.

"Julia!" Gaby said. Julia stood frozen on the stoop. She had no idea what to do. But Gaby handed the baby to her husband and wrapped her arms around Julia. She hugged her hard.

"This time of year is hard, I know," she whispered in Julia's ear. "But we have your back. You know that right?"

Julia found herself hugging Gaby back, tears spilling down her cheeks.

"Yes," Julia said. "I miss him. I miss him so much. But I have fruitcake."

The women laughed. "Come in," Gaby said, stepping aside. "I'm just, you know, nursing this damn baby for the eight thousandth time today. I swear, girl, my nipples are going to make a run for the hills."

"Maybe you'll get new ones for Christmas?" Julia said, with a giggle. Oh, she liked this Gaby! She really liked her! "I can't stay. I'm on my way home. Just wanted you to have a fruitcake. Because, like, I don't want a fruitcake and the thong people gave it to me."

Gaby took the cake and grinned. "We still on for tomorrow?" she asked.

"Yup," Julia said although she had no idea what Gaby was talking about.

"Great," said Gaby, hugging her again. "I love you. Go straight home. Call me when you get there."

"You're such a mom," Julia said.

"Oh my God," Gaby laughed. "I so am. I'm even annoying myself. I'll see you tomorrow." The door closed and, reeling, Julia stumbled down the brownstone steps.

"We're friends?" she asked Nick.

"BFF's," Nick said. "She took care of you when, you know, I died and all."

"A small act of kindness," she said. "Great impact."

Nick smiled at her. "Yes. You're getting it. And at some point the acts become second nature and not about our need to feel good about ourselves. It's a continuum. And now you're on it."

They were somewhere in the upper 80s and began drifting slowly back downtown. Nick seemed deflated, quiet, although it's hard to properly gauge the emotions of ghosts.

"So now what?" Julia asked. She was hungry and tired and thought she might have a slight hangover from the bottle of wine she chugged when Nick first showed up.

"Now we wait," Nick said.

"For what?"

"For the sun to come up."

"And?"

"And what?"

"How do we know it worked?" Julia yelled. "How do we know if I righted the right wrongs or whatever?"

"Stop yelling," Nick said. "You look like a crazy person."

"There's evidence to support the fact that I actually am a crazy person."

"Such drama," Nick said.

They walked in silence for a bit before Julia said, "Did you love me? Back when we were married, I mean."

"I thought I did," Nick said. "But I didn't really spend much time thinking about anything other than myself, to be honest."

"What changed?"

"I died."

"That's it?"

"What? That's not enough for you?"

"I…miss you," Julia said. Her heart, which she had always considered an efficient muscle designed to pump blood through her body, felt like a chasm. A look of pain drifted across Nick's see through face.

"What's the matter?" she asked.

"The sun," he said pointing to the east. "It's coming up. It's time for me to say good-bye."

"I don't want you to leave," she cried. "Please! Can you stay? I can do better. I know I can."

"I was only here to guide you along," Nick said. "Now it's time for me to rest. I'm very tired. Being dead is a lot of work."

"But...."

Nick's already vague outline wavered. "Remember Julia, keep your heart wide open."

"Nick!" But he was gone and all that remained in his place was a slight sheen to the snow piling up on the sidewalk.

CHAPTER 10

Standing on the corner, Julia was overcome with exhaustion. The first rays of Christmas morning light appeared, snaking around the buildings, pushing out the darkness. The snow had stopped and the sky was clear. After considering her situation, Julia did the only thing she could think to do: she headed for home.

"Merry Christmas," yelled a man cruising down the middle of Broadway on cross country skis.

"Merry Christmas," Julia croaked. Her voice was off, as if she'd spent all night in an airconditioned hotel room. Moments later, she passed the small coffee shop she frequented. The owner, a middle aged Indian man, waved to her as he unlocked his shop. She waved back. And her feet stopped.

"Good morning," she said to the man. He'd served her coffee every day for years and yet she didn't know his name. He looked startled.

"And to you as well," he said finally. "Do you celebrate this holiday?"

"Kind of," she said.

"Me too," the man nodded. "Kind of. I like the decorated trees. Would you care for some coffee this morning? You look...tired."

"I just spent the night with the ghost of my husband and I didn't get much sleep," she admitted. Instead of looking concerned, the man nodded gravely.

"That can do a person in," he said. "I'm Kishore."

"I'm Julia. It's nice to meet you."

Twenty minutes later, the sun was mostly up and Julia was on her way again, a steaming hot latte in her hand. Along the way, she searched for evidence that her future was different, that she'd chosen the right wrongs. But in truth she had no idea what she should be looking for.

When she arrived at her building, she stepped over a sleeping Lady Di and climbed the three flights of stairs to her apartment. Inside, everything looked the same. It was so quiet. Dust glimmered in the faint rays of sun. The framed picture of her and Nick sat on the mantle as it always had. She picked it up and stared at it. She had never really known him. Regret left her momentarily breathless. Tears spilled down her cheeks. Why had she been so blind?

Julia sat on the couch, latte in hand, feet crossed at the ankles. The silence squeezed in on her. The air felt thin and prickly. What had Nick said over and over? There's power in simple acts of kindness?

Suddenly, she was off the couch and running for the door. She took the stairs three at a time, practically falling down the last flight. Outside, Lady Di was propped up in the vestibule, yawning and stretching.

"Good morning," Julia said. It was so cold her breath made little puffy clouds.

"And to you," Lady Di said, her accent strong.

"It's Christmas," Julia said.

Lady Di looked around, surprised. "Really?"

"All day," Julia said. "I'd like to invite you up for breakfast. Nothing fancy. Will you come?"

Lady Di eyed her skeptically. "Me?"

"Yes. Please. We could both use some the company, right? Besides, it's cold out here."

The older woman shifted her bulk and rearranged her skirts, finally reaching out a hand for Julia to help her stand. But the vestibule was icy and covered in snow and as Julia pulled Lady Di up, her own feet went right out from under her. This was going to hurt.

But she didn't fall. A man's arms caught her from behind. At the same time, Lady Di grabbed Julia for support and now she was sandwiched between the unknown man and the princess.

"Well, this is awkward," the man said with a laugh. Oh, that laugh! That laugh! Her heart just about exploded at the sound.

"You're alive!" Julia untangled herself and turned to hug the man. But something in his eyes stopped her. He had no idea who she was.

"Please excuse me," she said, flustered. "I thought you were.... someone else." But inside, she was giddy with relief. Somehow, she'd gotten Nick another chance and she didn't care if she was still going to end up a sad lonely old lady who didn't even deserve cats. She'd made choices and those choices made a difference.

"I get that a lot," Nick said with a smile. "I'm pretty generic looking I suppose."

"No!" Julia said. "You're beautiful."

"Well, thank you for saying so," Nick said. "So what are you two lovely ladies doing on this wintery Christmas morning other than ice skating on the sidewalk?" Lady Di twittered and blushed at his attention.

"We were just going upstairs for some pancakes," Julia said. "Christmas pancakes. Would you...care to join us?"

"I was just heading out for a walk," Nick said. "Walking really clears the head. But who can resist pancakes? I'd love to join you."

"And maybe after we can walk together?" Julia asked, again breathless. Nick eyed her and for a flash Julia thought there was recognition. But it was fleeting. Nick broke into a broad smile.

"I'd love the company," he said. "It's a date."

Slowly, the odd trio made their way up the steps, Julia's hand under Lady Di's arm to keep her steady, Nick with his arm around Julia to give her support. And when Julia opened the door, the first thing she noticed was the mantle over the fake fireplace. It overflowed with photographs, all of a good life in progress.

"I love Christmas," Nick said, glancing around the neat apartment. "Don't you?"

"Yes," she said. "It's downright magical."

ABOUT THE AUTHOR

Elizabeth Maxwell is the internationally published author of several novels, including most recently Happily Ever After (Touchstone). She also writes under the name Beth McMullen. Visit Elizabeth MaxwellAuthor.com for information on Elizabeth's novels and sign up for the Wit's End Book Blog and Newsletter, a weekly discussion about great books trending right now.

ORION'S MIRROR

EVELYN G. WALKER

CHAPTER 1

As a girl, I loved stargazing with my father, even though at first I didn't know where to look. There was too much for my naked eye to handle. It wasn't until he bought me a telescope in eighth grade that I was able to decipher that vast, black sky into a navigable graph, each star frozen amongst its lot in the constellations. Up until then, I thought looking at the stars was like looking at a crowd, or a forest; my brain only saw the bigness of it.

But once I saw a few stars up close, I cared more about the whole thing. I liked that each star had a color and orientation, attracted and repelled other planets and stars, other bits of floating matter; each had a purpose. I didn't know it then, but this was my first glimpse into how people work. I'm not a fatalistic person, but I think I was supposed to understand the universe before I could handle my own life.

I am named after Halley's comet, which Mom and Dad saw together off the deck in their apartment when they were first married and still in grad school. They joke that's where I get the twinkle in my eye. Lately I've worked hard to keep this spark under control, to suppress it to a dormant, smoldering coal. I fed it too much last year, my senior year in high school — I became a fireball, and people got burned.

Tonight, in my quiet dorm room, the light is dim and uneven, which matches my mood. Finals begin tomorrow, and even though I'm mostly ready, this constant studying leaves me restless. I hear noises down the hall, and I turn up the volume on my speakers so I can't quite make out their voices, or their enthusiasm. I don't need that distraction.

I lean back to stretch and catch an uneasy funk from my armpits. My flannel pants have a coffee stain on the leg, from two days ago, which tells me I've worn them for the past two days, even to the dining hall downstairs. Now that classes are over prof's and TA's are holding office hours only, and I've pretty much holed up here. Haven't felt the sting of the cranky Boston winter. I'm really not taking great care of myself, but there's a purpose to it, there's a victory in here somewhere; this is my chance to prove myself. To restore the peace.

As if on cue, my phone buzzes and I look down to see Mom's name next to her tiny picture. She launches in, as she does.

"Halley, I'm glad I got you. I know you're busy but we need to talk holidays. We're hosting Christmas Eve, and Grandmother Jordan will be here, in your room. I invited Aunt Sue and Uncle Murray too..." Her voice is high and sharp. It almost flicks my ear over the phone.

"Mmm." I say.

"You need to send me your travel details so we know when to come get you from the airport. I might even need to send Justin. There's so much going on."

"Yep, okay, Mom, I will."

"Do that today, please." There's a distant click that sounds like she's setting down her pen. "And Halley, we're expecting a nice holiday together."

The pause is awkward, stretches out time into uncomfortably long seconds, creating a space like it's a physical thing. What do I even say to that?

"Mom, I am too. I know last summer things got out of hand, but..."

"I want to be clear about this."

"I'm getting good grades."

"No shenanigans."

"Mom, if you guys would just listen..."

"Well, your report card will do the talking for you, young lady. Finals start soon, right?"

I sigh and roll my eyes and kick my trash can under my desk all at the same time.

"Yep, tomorrow. I should get back to studying."

"That's my girl. Stick with it. All right then, you'll email that info tonight. We'll figure it out." The line disconnects but leaves her face, ghosted a sky blue, still eyeing me from the screen.

The idea of home is about as relaxing as an acid bath. I seriously miss its home-ness, the stuff that's tucked inside me like second nature, like the way you shove a hip into the center of the front door to close it completely. But the real ache, the yearning, the part I wish I could have back, comes from the role I was born with, that essential belonging, the years of Mom, Dad, me and my younger brother Justin knit together as a unit. Recently we've been broken apart, disassembled, and it's unclear if any pieces are missing, or if we'll even fit together neatly. So I guess going home no longer feels right. Somehow I fear I'll end up in a trap, airless and two-dimensional, a wildflower pressed into a book.

I turn back to my textbook. The first of my finals, Intro to Law in the Political Arena, is tomorrow morning. I think it will be tough, like really tough. This course is a requirement for my yet-undeclared major, Political Science, though I'm wavering on that. I like the course fine, but it doesn't stir me. I know the difference; I've had magical moments, where my synapses blaze, unable to stay contained; especially in Art History class, when the lights come down and the images explode before me, two stories high. In those moments, I am rapt. It's not fine.

Dad loves Poli Sci, thought I'd love it too — said it was a door-opener. He told me this back when he was still able to look me in the eye. I took the course for him.

I flip through my notes, and also those of my study partner, Luís. We swapped, and I'm glad we did — he picks up on different stuff than I do. Luís is an unlikely study buddy for me, given that his English is passable but not perfect; however he'll probably save my butt in this course. He's a sophomore from Venezuela, also an attorney's kid,

I suspect from a prominent family there. This stuff comes naturally to him, and his interest in me, which frankly feels more than platonic, comes in the form of a patient though unsolicited tutor. Not that I mind. Luís isn't like most guys I know; he's got some texture, like he's lived a life already. He's that guy — very tall, groomed, dark hair, shirts tucked in, brushed loafers. His cologne, while liberally applied, makes him smell older — like it could have wafted out of the men's room at my Dad's club. He has an easy laugh that comes from the barrel of his chest and shakes his shoulders. But he also has this incredible intensity, which I first found off-putting. His eyes consume my face when I talk, jumping from my eyes to my mouth. I suppose this could be because he's translating what I say, but it feels like I'm being studied. I've grown to like it, being somebody's subject.

Because when I stepped foot in Boston, I intentionally went invisible. It became my mission: to see what happened if I cut the bullshit and really tried. I've cranked the fun-meter down. I've kept away from the boys with their baseball caps and their ridiculous mustaches, the thumping parties up and down Fraternity Row, the girls entering a room in a cloud of perfume. I'm practically the opposite of many of the kids here - I'm discovering what I should have been.

Back at home, I was a miracle worker. There was an adrenaline rush I got from the shit I was able to pull off. It was a gift of mine, really; the instinctual ability to find the bare minimum threshold and live just above it. It used to drive Mom and Dad crazy. They are both so Type A, so organized, mechanical, precise. They were forever asking me if my homework was done, if my presentations were prepared, if I needed a second set of eyes. And my answer was always, as I raced past them to the driveway, where friends were waiting, a horn beeping impatiently, "I'm all good!" And since my grades held, they had no reason to press.

But my luck ran out last summer, and I promised myself that I'd be a new person here — that I'd had enough adventure to last some people a lifetime. It was time for the serious Halley, the one who had a plan. To reference my family playbook. By pure chance, I wasn't assigned a roommate, which is unusual for a freshman. So step one was accidental; I'm living a monk's life, in solace. I've preferred it, it's been my penance.

My restlessness suddenly goes exponential, and I know it's because home — my people, my life, my legacy — is looming. I stare at the phone and flick open the address book. I swipe slowly, knowing where I'll end up, but in no hurry to get there. When I see her name my heart falters. It's been four months since we've talked. I press the button. After several rings, I hear the rasp to her voice, so familiar, so distant. For more than a decade I heard it every day.

"Well, if it isn't Halley." I picture her in her TV room, where she zones out most evenings. Her hair is dark brown, near black, and spills over her shoulders and onto the back of the sofa in thick, unruly waves. Her body is haphazard, one leg up, one down. She holds the phone lightly to her face, which looks stern, partly because she has a strong nose, but also from the perennial dark circles under her eyes, both hereditary from her strong Italian lineage.

"Hi Risa." My voice is loud even to my ears. I can't think of where to start. "How's everything?"

She chuckles, "I'm good, I guess. I'm here, but I'm good."

I nod, the hushed room spreading absently around me. "I'm coming back next week. Didn't know if you'd be around…" The insincerity in this rings like an alarm. Of course she's home. We both know her family's holiday traditions, etched like runes in our history together; I've been at her house for many of them. All of her relatives gather there: men crowd the balconies, leaning heavily on railings and smoking; stoves bubble over with the family's traditional Struffoli cookies; the elder aunties settle in the parlor, their mid-calf skirts lined up, sheltering their crossed ankles and sensible black shoes. The noise level is deafening. It's a magical thing.

"Cool, yep, sure." She says this loosely, so the words swim around us, unanchored.

"How's Nonna?" She's my favorite, very old, and very brittle with everything but her words. She speaks fire.

"You know Nonna. She's always into something, like a child." I can hear her smiling. "Her latest is poker. She won't leave me alone."

For some reason, this is the sucker punch. I miss her so much I can feel the absence, taste the alienation. "Risa, I'm so sorry about everything. I wish I could undo it."

"Hmm, yeah. Halley, me too. But it is what it is." Her voice unexpectedly springs with levity, "God, that expression sucks. It's totally useless."

"Could I swing by when I'm home? What would…" I can't even finish the sentence.

"I don't know, Halley. Try me when you get here. We'll see."

I regret everything about this, this biggest on my shortlist of life's real regrets. The conversation ends abruptly like it started — familiar but unresolved, a life interruption, like the pause button was pressed and we're frozen mid-frame, across from each other.

The last time I saw her we were both wearing suits, in Judge Reimert's courtroom, and our attorneys wouldn't allow us to speak to each other. It was the scariest day of my life.

I went up first, and fortunately had Jim McCready as my attorney. My father called him 'The Beast,' and the first time I saw Jim, leaning casually against the window frame in my father's office, I understood why. Jim had played football in college and was still physically immense, with the tightly reigned intensity of a linebacker now neatly packaged in a navy suit, the slight pucker of his jacket indicating a hand-sewn seam. He didn't blink much, not even when I blurted out the story; that we had 'borrowed' the brown '74 Chevy Nova parked alongside the park; that we'd found it unlocked with the keys on the dash and it just seemed like a funny idea at the time; that it was my idea, and Risa had relented and said she should probably drive, because her older brothers had taught her to drive a stick-shift like a boss. Jim stopped me then with his hazel eyes, smallish in his tawny face, and held up a giant hand, gold pinky ring leading, and said, "Only yours. I don't want her story. Only yours." I knew then how this was going down.

The proceeding was mechanical. When I took the stand, Jim stood motionless before me, except for the occasional smoothing of his tie. His voice was surprisingly quiet, which I recognized as a tactical move, because the room stilled to hear him. I answered his questions using as few words as possible, as he'd coached. The story unfolded, him coaxing the details and managing the narrative - I was a spirited, talented young woman, headed off to a top college in the fall, misdirected by a wayward moment but still on track.

And for me it closed quietly; I paid my fines, was counseled all summer by a young social worker named Linden alongside her waxy begonias, did six weeks community service cleaning up parks as restitution. Then I packed up and went to Boston for college in the fall. I was whole. The Jordan family was intact.

Risa's family had no money, so she got a public defender named Larry. Larry wore broad ties, and dark leather shoes with rubber soles that squeaked as he walked.

Risa is six months older than me, and was tried as an adult. As the driver, she was convicted of joyriding and spent a month in county prison.

Risa is now living at home on probation, where her future is trapped with her.

I stand up and toss the notebook to the ground. Grabbing my coat and stuffing my feet into boots, I pull a fleece skullcap low across my forehead, so it hugs my ears and covers my unbrushed, unwashed hair, a limp, brown carpet-fringe resting on my shoulders. It's time for some air.

The night is bracingly cold, and my cheeks feel the sting first. Wind cuts through my thin pajama bottoms but there's a strange release that comes as I tense up, bearing inward. It feels good to relinquish to bigger things, like the depth of winter's night.

I walk around a corner and step onto a stone pathway, away from the dorm's flood lights and the main road's street lamps, and shift my head upward, to the midnight sky. There are white clusters of clouds, cirrus, I think, that appear almost luminescent, as though they create their own heat and light. Once I am deeper down the path, there's a gentle sloping hill with tall trees off in the distance and a lawn that stretches to the next dorm. I pause there as my eyes adjust, and the stars begin firing; they are hot white, flickering blue, pink and yellow to the periphery.

Dad says my name inexorably ties me to greatness, to the cosmos. We used to call ourselves students of the stars, Dad and I. We'd bundle up, and go out on our freezing deck, then lean together, shoulders and temples touching, merging our sight line. I'd follow his finger as he'd pick a constellation and give me its story. "Now that one, Halley, it's so bright it looks like a star but it's more like a cluster. That's Pleiades, about 400 light years away. It's a loose open cluster of young, hot blue stars." And beneath his glasses I'd see his eyes smiling. "Marvelous, right? They're essentially teenagers, like you." He'd pat my back. "Bright future." I'd chuckle and lean in closer.

I shiver. The cold has spread to the inside, and I realize that looking back doesn't give me any warmth. It freezes me in my tracks. It's time to move on. I turn back to the dorm, to the new Halley, the fresh star who is white hot and cruising at a speed of 150 miles per hour, not looking back at the trail of debris she's left in her orbit.

CHAPTER 2

Exam week is over and now I feel lame, stunned by a bone-leaching tiredness. It really was a battleground, six exams over five days. I think I did fine. I'm not walking around chest bumping anyone, but I can certainly live with myself. I may even have kicked some ass.

There's a hard sleet outside, which isn't ideal for a travel day. The sky is heavy and thick. The brake lights and windshield wipers are frantic along the turnpike, though the cars move slowly, sluggish and hesitant in the crowd. It appears all Boston inhabitants are leaving this Friday afternoon also.

Luís is sharing my cab to Logan. He's visiting some relatives over the holiday in Miami instead of going all the way home to Venezuela. His exam earlier today was in Cultural Anthropology, where I think the language gap was possibly a real problem. I feel guilty that I haven't helped him as much as he's helped me.

"I'm sure you did fine." I say.

He's sulking against his car door, his face slack with dismay, manspeading his legs across two-thirds of the backseat. He smacks the vinyl seat on either side of him, "Who cares the differences between Franz Boas and E.B. Tylor? They are the same, both idiots. Studies of stupidity."

I try not to look at him. I'm amused by his tantrum, which he probably won't appreciate. "Luís, we have some time before our planes leave. Let's get shitty at the airport."

He nods. "Yes, Halley. This time you are right."

I stumble through the airport lines like a zombie, shuffling my feet. Dead eyes. Craving something but I don't know what. The airport is thickly packed, crowded with currents moving in all directions. As I enter the terminal, the melee absorbs me in full holiday assault, the cheerful music streaming out of three-sided stores, slick shopping bags balanced carefully on wheelie suitcases.

I find Luís at a seafood place, and we sit in the corner of the bar on high stools, pushed so close together our legs occasionally touch. There's a bright fish mural behind the server. Luís orders oysters and martinis, even though the idea of this meal followed by a plane ride makes me nervous. I'm not a great flyer to begin with.

He holds up his glass to toast. "So here we are, finished with the semester. Having food and drink together. Is this a date?"

I sputter and shake my head, vodka spraying in a fine mist. I'm definitely not playing this cool. "I don't know. Who asked who?"

"It does not matter. Salúd. To one ending, one beginning." He drinks, then takes an oyster and slurps it, chewing the final bite, looking at me. I'm starting to feel a little loose, like my jowls have gone numb and my fingertips are tingly.

We laugh about the week, and at one point I rest my hand on his arm and lean in. His smell is strong, as always — leather, smoke, and something else sharp to the nose. It feels nice to let go a little, getting close to him, opening the aperture a little to some fun. Harmless enough.

He leans across me for a cocktail napkin, and when he returns the stubble on his cheekbone grazes my cheek. I feel prickly heat rising in my chest and face, and I sense he can see it - I rock a mean blush.

"Are you sad you're not going home?" I ask. Our faces are now very close.

"I am not sad." He says. He tucks a strand of my hair behind my ear. "My family will always be there."

His words send an aftershock through me. I'm the one going home, but have an empty, hollow pit in my stomach. Dread. I don't know how this will go. Before I left for school, my family didn't seem to know how to behave around me, so we all just receded. Dad made excuses to eat dinner near the courthouse. Mom and Justin were around, but treated me with a deprecated kindness, in the spectrum of pity and politeness. There was a distance to it, all the words unspoken but still drifting around the room, watching us, haunting me.

"My family is really, really messed up right now," I say. "And it's all my fault. I'm a train wreck."

"No, no, no, querida. Not you." And he leans in quickly for the softest, sweetest kiss, a puff of air wrapped in velvet. I almost missed it. "You're the train. Nothing will stop you."

It feels like something Risa would have said to me, about us. I feel an old rush, like something is expanding me from the inside, stretching me bigger and greater. Unstoppable. I miss these feelings. Speed. Impulse. Need.

I reach over and pull his face close to mine and I kiss him, firmly. Our noses press into each other and I feel him breathe in sharply. Even with my eyes closed I know he's smirking. It feels happy and a little bit hungry, like we're trying to break off a piece of the moment and swallow it whole before we say good-bye tonight.

I'm no stranger to a row of shot glasses, but Luís and I collect quite a few before I warn him we're about to miss our flights. We kiss again, a hasty and messy mash-up, in the middle of the busy terminal. As I head to my gate I can't stop grinning. My chin is tender, tangible proof of desire; I'm glad he left me with this little reminder, so that no matter how things go at home tonight, tomorrow and the next day I can touch my face and remember what it's like to feel wanted.

I arrive at my gate to a sign flickering red, which tells me that my flight is delayed, as they all seem to be, so I find a spot alongside a side far wall and slump down, my backpack resting against my thighs. The rain beats on the windows wearily, as the airport crew directs traffic below in their slickers and orange vests. I put on my headphones and lean back, an insuppressible smile fixed on my face, and replay the evening.

I look up and realize my headset is silent. The airport is still swollen with people, but the windows are black. I hold up my phone and it's dead. The gate across from me, my gate, is loosely packed with weary-looking travelers, jackets draped across their bodies, a toddler asleep in his stroller with his legs dangling over the side. I dig through my bag and find a phone charger and spot an outlet not far away. I plug in and wait for the screen to light up. After seemingly endless minutes, it fires up. It's 11PM. The message lights flare.

My tongue feels like lead in my mouth.

First a text from Justin: 8:30PM. I'm here, circling. Flight landed. Where RU? Lose yr bag? Call me.

Oh sweet Jesus. I switch over to voicemail.

6:30PM. Mom. "Halley, your flight is delayed so we're going to have dinner without you. I'm sending Justin to the airport. He'll wait at the curb downstairs. Look for him when you land."

9:00PM. Mom. "Young Lady, what the hell is going on? Did you miss your flight? Why aren't you answering your phone? I'm paging you."

10:00PM. Dad. "Halley, it's ten o clock. This is ridiculous. We don't know what's happened. Go back to your dorm. We don't need this. I guess we'll talk in the morning.

While I'm reading, a text comes through from Luís: 11:05PM. Hola, guapa. In Miami, thinking about you. Text me when you get this, anytime is fine.

I yank the cord out of the wall and throw my bag over my shoulder. My hands are shaking. I'm in for a long night.

CHAPTER 3

The drive home inside the car is silent. The pavement seams make a repeating sound under Dad's sedan, rhythmic like a mantra. It's all I can hear above the pounding in my chest.

The sun has just come up and the winter sky has an orange cast to it. The moon is low and bright on the horizon. Waning, I think, how ironic.

Dad grips the steering wheel at ten and two, his fingers occasionally unfolding then returning, finger by finger, to their places. His face is unreadable, but not in a relaxed, happy way; his cheeks indent beneath his high cheekbones, leaving flesh pooling toward his jawline, heavy and weighted; his lips are pursed tightly, and his greying stubble points in all directions.

"Dad, it was an accident, I don't know what else to say. I fell asleep. I was right there." His face is impassive. I can't tell if he's listening. "I was just so tired after finals…" Still nothing. I look out the window and say quietly into the car's steamy, cold, morning air. "It's not that big of a deal."

He snaps toward me. "Not a big deal? Do you know how worried we were? We didn't know what the hell happened." After a beat he speaks again, a bit defeated. "And you smell like a drunk from the back of the bus, Halley. I don't know what to do."

My spine compresses with the weight of it all. There's nothing to say. They're not going to cut me a break. There is no trust, no comfort here. Not after all the studying, all the sacrifice. That doesn't seem to matter. They see me through a different lens now, and I bear the burden of proof.

I've seen Dad like this before, but only once, that night the police brought me in after Risa and I took the Nova for a spin. They'd fingerprinted us, took our information, then put us in a small cell. There were three other women in there, all older. I had the impression that particular cell hadn't seen many other high school students in tank tops and gladiator sandals.

Dad was wearing a plaid button-down shirt when they brought me to him, his khaki pants held up loosely by a brown leather belt. His hair was disheveled, like he may have been in bed reading.

"Halley, what is going on here?" he asked, more indignant than curious.

"Dad, I'm so glad to see you!" I ran forward. "Are Risa's parents here too?"

He shook his head incredulously. "I have no idea. Did I hear this correctly? Did you girls steal a car?" He takes off his glasses and rubs his eyes. "Do you know what you've done?"

It's that look of disgust that gets to me. I've seen him tired, irritated, even baffled before. But only twice in my eighteen years have those eyes been trained on me with full-on rancor. Like I've caused pain and offense. Today is number two.

My eyes feel heavy and the movement of the car lulls me, but I dare not fall asleep. We sit in more silence, me waiting for his next move. I imagine he's hoping that I'll stop moving altogether.

Mom steps out onto the front stoop when we arrive. She doesn't run down the three stairs to greet me, or help with my bags. She waits, her arms folded across each other, her hip resting lightly against the black wrought-iron railing. Her hair is done and her make-up is on. She looks pissed. Dad slips past her, making brief eye contact, stepping inside without looking back.

I grab my giant bag out of the trunk and make my way up the stairs. "Hi Mom." I say quietly.

"Halley." Her hands go to her hips, fists in tight balls. "What on earth?"

"It's nothing, there's no story. I'm sorry."

She stands still for a beat. Her eyes roll, so dramatically her head actually tilts with them. She jerks one arm forward and squeezes my forearm. It reminds me a bit of when I was scolded as a child, but strangely I'm reassured by her touch. "You're exhausted." Some of the chill has left her voice. "We'll talk later. Go rest, you have your room for tonight."

I wheel my bag through the entry and up the stairs to my room. I nudge the door mostly closed and roll my bag behind it, like a bookend. I want to slam the door and throw my body against it. But I can't block them out completely.

In this room I feel more like myself again. I flop on my bed. I knew coming home would feel like moving upstream, forging forward despite the pressure, constant and unrelenting, to move backward. But here's something else unexpected; relief. The texture of my bed-spread — the one I picked out when I was thirteen, with the eyelet tiered ruffle - is rough like I remember it, the warp and weave made of thready polyester. But it's mine, and there's a slight dusty musk that seeps from my pillow when I lay down that smells like the real me, the one that swells with excitement and fear and boredom and love.

There's a gentle tap at my door before Justin pushes his head through the crack. He looks noticeably different, his face longer, his shoulders fuller, even after a few short months. His reddish blonde hair, a color that traces from Mom's lineage, is recently shaved, so that only a tiny bit of fuzz shades his scalp.

"Tweet, tweet. Hey, jailbird." His voice is taunting, and his sly smile twists me up. He gave me that nickname last summer. Of course it infuriates me, but the last thing I'll do is show it. "Welcome home. Can I come in?"

"Whatever, jackass." I watch him struggle as he pushes open the door, knocking over my giant suitcase with a loud thump on the car-pet as he enters the room. He pulls out my desk chair and sits down, crossing one ankle over the other knee, picks at a toenail.

"So… you're back. Interesting start." He looks up at me, his face blooming with mischief.

"Seriously? Off me. Mom and Dad are enough."

"Yeah but no show last night? Big move." He chuckles. "I'm glad you're home, Halley. Things are boring around here without you. Just didn't think you'd go for broke on your first night."

I stare at him and gesture toward the door.

He doesn't leave but rather settles in, leans back, all awkward elbows and knees. He looks like a daddy longlegs spider. "I'll bet you're raging at school, right? I can't wait to hear — two more years here, but then I'm out, just like you. You're free."

"Nope," I say, "it's not like that. I'm busting ass. I've never worked this hard before. I'm telling you, college is a different league."

"Dah. Save the 'studying' bullshit for Mom and Dad. I know you, Halley. You're an animal. You can tell me."

I stare at him and viscerally remember what it was like when I first got my license at sixteen, when I had that first taste of freedom. How I left the house at any chance. I snuck out late at night, I lied about my whereabouts. I let go of the rules, just to prove I could. But that joyride, those thirty minutes that Risa and I were behind that noisy, rumbling Nova engine, sitting airily on the grey leather bench seat, completely enthralled by our gall, our buoyancy, the windows rolled down and freedom whipping through our hair, we knew only the thrill of our racing pulses and trembling adrenaline; we forgot that it was all temporary. That freedom was a right, a privilege, that was generously granted but could be swiftly lost, or worse. Taken.

"Justin, you may not believe this, but I'm done with that. Last summer changed me. These kids at my school? Every one was top of their class. They're all used to winning, every time." I shrug. "I've been knocked down a peg, but I needed it. I'm telling you, I'm different."

"You look a little different, I can see it in your eyes," he says, standing and heading toward the door. "But you don't smell different. Take a shower, Jailbird."

I'm parked down the street from her house watching the usual chaos — cars parked on her lawn and driveway, neglected front door standing open despite the brisk Pennsylvania air. You can hear the chatter from a few houses down, pulsing, and I wonder if their emphatic, Italian hands are actually pushing the sound waves out that open front door.

I stand by the car for a moment where I know nobody can see me. Risa and I were separated, wrenched apart really, after the arrest. My father forbade me to talk to her until after the trial. For two weeks she still called, and her parents even drove over and suggested on our doorstep that our families needed to be together, to help each other, during this difficult time. They had no idea that the Jordan view of family had firmer limits than the Puccinelli's.

But for those same reasons, they're a part of me. I grew up with them. Risa and I befriended way back in second grade, badged and bonded together as Brownies; sisters that neither of us had at home. She was simply always near me, for as long as I remember. And so my loss feels more than just losing my ally, my sister — there's a piece of me, a good piece, that's imbedded in her and her family. Us adrift, not talking or laughing or crying through the whole mess, was probably more troubling than my parents shipping me off in shame. I know the rhythms of my family's love, but escaping the Puccinelli's, walking away like a refugee who abandons a miserable country, wasn't right. I have to know; have to rip open this barely sutured wound that's healed horribly, oozing with malfeasance and fault. This absence of us, incomplete and neglected, is not our ending. As I start walking toward Risa's house, I know it's time to break us back open and start a new recovery, one way or the other.

It feels strange to knock, since the door is totally ajar, and one year ago I would march in and greet the extended relatives on my own. So I ring the bell and wait awkwardly as it reverberates through the household, escalating shouts throughout. I hear Risa's brother, Matteo, three years older than us, shouting "I got it!" as he approaches the half-closed door.

"Woah, Halley. What are you doing here?" He steps outside and pulls the door closed behind him.

I'm so nervous my thoughts are completely scrambled. "Oh Matteo I'm happy it's you, I wanted to see Risa and all of you and I probably should have called but I was afraid you'd say no and I seriously can't imagine being home for the holidays and not seeing you guys and I feel so rotten and empty. I just really want to talk to Risa." I choke this out, my mouth dry and tactile like sandpaper.

Matteo jerks his head over his shoulder toward the door, oddly, several times, like a nervous tick, before I realize he hears activity inside the house. As he opens his mouth to respond, the door flies open again, and Nonna Puccinelli stands in the doorway, her green apron hanging loosely from her neck, her hair, dyed between red and purple, dusted with white flour.

"Halley?" She cries out, as the front of the house suddenly hushes.

"Nonna," I falter, "It's so good to see you. I'm so sorry about everything." My head hangs down and tears flood my eyes. "Is Risa free? Can I see her?"

Her forehead bends in half, eyebrows tilting outward, her entire face wracked with grief. "Ah Halley." She calls me her daughter in Italian as she pushes Matteo out of the way — she cups her hand to my cheek and gives it a gentle slap, and it stings but she holds it there. Then she grapples with my sweater and reaches around me for a hug, pressing me into her arms and chest, owning me for the moment. I'm off balance for a second, as though falling, stunned but relieved to be here again. She pulls back and whispers horsely in my ear, "Risa loves you. All is not right, but does not have to be so wrong. Go to her. Tell her what you feel, she needs to know." She releases me and gives me a gentle shove. "Go, she's downstairs."

I walk through the house, feeling shamed and raw, like I'd stepped in nude. The aunties are in the parlor across from the stairs, quietly staring. I cross through the hallway, with the family's framed photos watching me across generations, and step through the doorway that leads to the basement. The air is very cold. I can hear Risa's father and uncles chatting down below and I realize they're making their holiday sausages. Risa always works the back of the line with a barbaric-looking device, a wooden dowel with nails driven through it, which they cleverly call the poker, as it aerates the sausages to allow them to dry, to release the pressure. I'd done it alongside her for many years.

There are bright fluorescent lights hanging from the low ceiling, and the back wall is draped with links of reddish sausages, dangling from rows of nails. As I descend, all eyes turn to watch the newcomer. I continue and the sound of my footsteps bounces off the concrete walls.

Risa's father Lucca steps forward. From the back of the room Risa calls out, "It's okay, Dad," and makes her way around the assembly table covered with white butcher paper, crowded with piles of freshly ground meat and long, translucent casings; she walks behind the staggered row of her uncles who have stopped their grinding and stuffing, who watch her silently as she crosses; she reaches the base of the steps and looks up at me. She's wearing a long-sleeved t-shirt with a centaur print on the front, and she seems smaller, though it's hard to tell if she's lost weight or I'm just intimidated by the room. Her hair is tangled in a messy bun.

"Hi Sonrisa," I say. It comes out without even thinking. It's an old nickname I gave her, meaning smile in Spanish. I stammer. "It's, I hope it's okay I'm here, that I stopped by. I just...hoped to see you for a minute."

She turns past me and heads up the stairs. I follow. She heads directly out the front door, away from all the watching eyes, and says finally on the front driveway, "You drove right? Let's take a spin."

We climb into the car and as I'm closing my door a thought hits me — the last time we were alone in a car, things went horribly wrong. I turn to her, "Where do you want to go?"

"Anywhere," she says, "away from here."

I pull away. She's looking out the far window. Introspective. I drive out of her neighborhood, where the homes are packed closely together, separated by cracked, paved driveways and partially mowed lawns. I finally speak up. "Risa, I don't even have words to tell you how sad and sorry I am."

"It's really beautiful out tonight," she says, tenderness in her voice. "I forgot how pretty this town is when everyone puts out their decorations. I guess I haven't noticed it all tricked out." She glances toward me. "Remember how we used to mix up the Santas from people's yards? How mad they'd get when we'd swap them?" She laughs. "We never got caught. Man, that was funny."

"It was ridiculous."

"Yeah, I've thought a lot about the shit we used to do."

"I think about it too. God, I'm so sorry."

Her face brightens briefly under the streetlights, then goes back to shadow. "I'm not," she says. "We made a lot of harmless trouble, we messed up once. Even then, it could have been much, much worse. This sounds crazy, but I'm okay it worked out the way it did. You got into a great school, and you got to go; I was going to Community College anyway. When you stop and think about it, nothing really changed."

I can't wrap my head around what I'm hearing. Is it possible she doesn't see me as a villain, a coward, a turncoat? That we're still the same girls we've been for a decade, with new notches carved into our belts. That she just gets me. I notice the car is decelerating as I struggle for breath. I pull over into a 24 hr gas station parking lot, roll down the window and breathe deeply into the cold. My lungs only seem to fill to half capacity so I heave, over and over, trying to fill them.

I wonder if this is the breakdown that I've been waiting for, if this is the moment when I fully crack from all of it: the trying, the reinventing, the persuading, the pushing, the hiding, the crying.

Risa leans over and rubs my shoulder. "Slow down, Halley. Stop. You're hyperventilating. You're going to be okay."

"Are. We. Okay?" I blubber, gasping, unsure if she can even understand me.

"This is us. What can I say? You and me, we live big. It's sucked for a few months, don't get me wrong, but it'll settle."

She has a meek smile on her face. I weep.

"My probation's almost done. I was always going to work for my uncle anyway, right? See, it's cool." She points at me. "But don't bail on me again. That was what really hurt."

I get out of the car and walk over to Risa's side, where she opens up, climbs out, and we tangle in a hug, long and close, rocking a bit side to side to the holiday music piping from the outside speakers.

CHAPTER 4

Christmas Eve is always the night that tips Mom over the edge, the night she prepares the feast that Dad grew up with, the traditional Polish Wigilia. Because it has so many courses of seafood and then also the borscht, the pierogi, the poppyseed cakes — she fusses in the kitchen industriously for several days leading up to Christmas. Either that or she hovers in the laundry room over the ironing board heavily starching and pressing her own family's traditional Irish lace. Either way, Christmas Eve is always the night when one small thing — a burned dish, a dripping gravy boat — sends her reeling. So we stay out of her way until she beckons.

Normally I'm her number two, the one to whom she barks orders. But today she asked Justin to run to the store to do the last-minute shopping. She asked my father to pull down the platters from the top shelf of the pantry. She herself managed the timer, juggling which trays were in and out of the oven. I imagined that the family had just tightened up without me, the elastic cinched closer; but rather than feeling left out, I felt a bit of latitude, that I'd already served my round of duty and maybe was better suited elsewhere.

I go out to sit with my relatives in the living room, on the cream sofas with a slight sheen to their floral pattern, a room normally neglected except for piano lessons or holidays. There my Grandmother Jordan, my father's mother, a conservative former grammarian, sits with my Aunt Sue and Uncle Murray, my mother's sister and brother-in-law, both childless and currently the proprietors of a small English Pub near Amish country, all discussing the weather predictions for Christmas Day. When I enter, the conversation tapers off.

"So tell us, Halley, how's that school of yours up in Boston?" Murray asks.

"You liking it?" Sue says.

"It's going well, but so tough. Way harder than last year. I just finished finals." I give a hopeful smile.

"Well, surely that's not saying much." Grandmother's face is tipped up, challenging me, the loose flesh forming a wattle on the front her neck; she's crowing like a rooster.

"I'm sorry, what was that, Grandmother?"

"Hmph, Halley, you heard me. A young lady such as yourself does not change her ways, she merely changes direction. I believe that may apply here."

"Now I don't think that's fair," Sue interrupts. "Halley…"

Murray pipes up, "I agree, she was cleared from all that. We have to give her a chance."

I think about what they may have said about me when I was not in the room. That I was impetuous, out of control, a familial risk. And yet. There's more in me that I've unearthed over this last semester, more substance, more depth, which I know now from sitting amongst the best, and feeling scared but not lost, knowing that I had something to offer. That I was more than the fun.

"I own it." I say, my voice a little loud in the low-ceilinged, formal room. "I fucked things up last summer, and I've taken responsibility for it." I look to my Grandmother, "I'm sorry, but it's how I feel. I made a small, dumb move, but I learned something too. I learned that it's not enough to push against nothing. You have to have something real in this world that you accomplish, that you love. That's what I'm finding now. And it doesn't matter what you think."

"You can't address me with that tone or that language, young lady. I told your father the same thing when he was your age."

And that's when I realize. All this time, I felt like I had to carve out my own territory to be noticed, to fit neatly in this ecosystem in which I felt unsubstantial, like I was the air, clawing for my own space and density. But in reality they needed me for every breath. I just had to be myself.

"You don't deserve that, Grandmother, you're right. But I am who I am, and I keep getting better. That's what I've come to know. Maybe Dad and I aren't so far apart after all."

We've missed each other's calls over the past few days, but the wires have been hot between Luís and I. He's been sending me funny text messages; nothing too naughty, but just zesty enough that I keep my phone on me at all times. It's been good to have an entertaining sidebar.

My phone rings just as I've set the table in the dining room. Everyone else is either in the kitchen or sitting in the front room, so I steal away to the family room in the back of the house. I keep the lights off.

"Luís, hi, I'm here!" I whisper-speak.

"Guapa!" His voice booms. He's clearly had a few mojitos with the relatives down in Miami.

"Hey there." I wag my hands for him to keep the volume down, as if he could see me. I actually wish Luís could see me. My face is cracked open into a smile. I can't help it. "Happy Christmas Eve! What are you up to?"

"Ahhh, querida," he shouts over music in the background, "we are enjoying life! I'm wishing you were here as my dance partner, we would paint this town red and green." He laughs hilariously at himself.

I reach over to the bookshelf and pull down a framed picture. It's Risa and I, probably about nine years old. We are perky in short-shorts, giant grins misshapen by jagged teeth, arms wrapped possessively over each other's shoulders. That was what optimism looked like. But Luís's laughter over this phone is what optimism feels like now. It's confident, and hopeful, it's accepting but demanding; it seeks to make others happy but knows that happiness really starts inside your deepest kernel, the part of you that's half light and half dark, where all the potential lives.

"Merry Christmas, Luís. I'll see you in a week."

"A week! Dios mío, it's too long."

I chuckle. "You'll blink and we'll be back. Go outside and look for me in the stars."

"I see you, Halley. I'm outside and you are everywhere. Merry Christmas."

Plates are being cleared from the table and Mom is organizing the washing and drying stations in the kitchen for her china. The meal ultimately was lovely, and the conversation returned to benign chatter about mass tomorrow and the Eagles, both of which elicited many opinions around the table. There was a delightful sense of predictability to it — a delicious feast that was graciously received; some shared words and reflections to commemorate the year that had passed since the last Wigilia; and the tumult that accompanied the disassembly of the annual tradition. I felt sated.

I slipped out the sliding doors onto the deck and was surprised to see Dad out there in the far corner, fiddling with the telescope, which had been sitting, covered and dusty, in the garage for several years.

"I thought we should get this out again," he said, his face hovering above the eyepiece, his hands making familiar adjustments along the lower mounts and the focus tube.

"What do you see?" I asked, part of our old routine.

"I see it all," he said, "it's a clear, cloudless night. You only get these in winter." He leaned into the telescope and shifted his shoulders to pivot it around.

I looked up also to the giant sky, and could appreciate the complexity of it, that the matter made clusters, which became stars, which formed constellations, which created galaxies. All of it moving, exploding, growing. All of it connected.

"Let's look at Orion," I said, "it's always been my favorite."

"Mine too," he says, "It's an obvious choice, but it's so powerful in the sky, an icon really; historically it's been a navigation anchor across civilizations."

"Sometimes I have to stop, look really close at one thing so when I zoom out again, I have more appreciation for what I'm seeing. You know what I mean?" I close one eye and settle into the telescope, controlling my breathing to a slow, even exchange; I focus slowly, watching the stars morph from wooly fingerprints to clear pinpricks in the black sky.

"I do," he says. "I understand."

I shift away and step back so he can see. As he approaches, he leaves a hand, warm and connected, at my hip. "I'm glad we still have this," I say, placing my hand over his. "I like that we share this together."

"We share a lot, Halley. You and I are like two sides of a reflection. Not exactly alike, but one feeding off of the other. I've always felt like I just knew you, and I guess I've felt so lost recently. You changed, and it's taken me a bit to find you again, to refocus on that same girl that's stamped in the cosmos. You've always been one the brightest stars, you just changed color."

He doesn't see me smile in the darkness, but we both feel a familiar warmth seeping into the dark cold. I lean my shoulder into his and give him a nudge.

ABOUT THE AUTHOR

Evelyn G. Walker writes short stories, and is currently working on a novel. She lives in the Bay Area with her husband, two kids and a dog. (He's a rescue, a boxador, in case you're curious.) You can contact her at evelyn.walker1234@gmail.com.

NOT EVEN A MOUSE

SPRING WARREN

It was a whiningly cold winter in the ill-named town of Fiji, Dakota Territory. Chocked with gray skies, mud underfoot, and stretches of time good for nothing but polishing boredom, it seemed an unending season. I rented a room in a boarding house serving single men that simmered with enough loneliness and bluster that fistfights broke out with the regularity we all wished our bowels possessed. I was pressed into a single room that I suspected had in better times been a closet as there was not enough room for the mattress. The thin pad, hardly more than cardboard and ticking, steepled against the wall at one end. This provided a foyer of sorts for the mice that darted in and out of a little hole in the wall to stare at me. Even they pitied my situation.

Worse, I'd run out of money and faced eviction. I suspected my sweetheart, Phaegin–who managed her life and the Fiji hotel with the efficiency of a cleric–was beginning to think less of me, with my complaints and my volatile health. She was yet sweet to me, sure— "Ah, Neddy, we've been through thick and thin together, haven't we though?" she'd said—but the truth of it was we'd been through nothing but thin. I'd taken her from the cream life in Connecticut, where she'd been poised to marry a fine fellow with a finer bank account. I was the bomb that went off in her life. We'd had to hightail it from the law, and also from ease, comfort, culture, and the wedding to a life she deserved.

"Ah yeah, Ned. I deserve more," she'd agree with me. "I should have roast beef and sugar pie every day. But I've got you, and it's kept me from getting fat."

I thought Phaegin would look very good indeed round as an apple, though. Her boss at the Fiji Hotel seemed to agree. Randall Allan paid her more than the going wage, and gave her a work chair with a flowered cushion. He gazed at her with eyes more fitting a cow than a businessman.

Oh, I could see where this was going. If I wanted to keep my Irish rose I'd better act soon. Christmas was coming, and I told myself that the holiday was the perfect time to ask for Phaegin's hand. If I didn't pledge my troth, I worried that Randall Allan would pledge his. Which meant I desperately needed some troth to pledge. I needed a stake, and a ring, and some measure of certainty that I could give Phaegin a life she deserved.

I, with great fervor, searched for a job; but no respectable position was to be had in the tiny muddy town of Fiji.

With my standards dropping like mercury, I finally found employ with a shady distiller named Wraque.

Wraque distilled what he called whiskey and others called moonshine, and still others a means to murder. My job was to lubber the leftover ferment from the rough distillery—a small room clamped up with fumes—into the pig sty behind the building that stunk even more than the rotting rye and barley.

Mine was a short-lived employ with Wraque, for within a week the florid man lit a match, ignited the toxins rising from the still and blew the windows out of the building. Wraque was lucky to escape with his life, but he did forfeit every hair on his head and face, which made him look something like an earthworm thereafter as it never grew back.

Now bankrupted, Wraque gave me a barrel of raw alcohol in recompense for my week's work that at a rip-roaring 90 proof was better suited for tanning leather and peeling paint from metal than drinking.

I hatched a plan to utilize the noxious alcohol to good profit. As it was the barrel of hooch was worth less than five dollars to someone anxious to lose their senses to a night of belting back rotgut. But if I were to use the spirits to make cordials I figured I could sell the stuff in small bottles and make a goodly profit.

Once a member of well-heeled society I was knowledgeable of liqueurs, cordials, and apertif. Quality concoctions render the triple experience of warmth, coolness, and tingling by sophisticated mixtures of herbs and fruit. For my Dakota elixir I used elderberry—which grew like weed on the streambeds—deeply wizened off-color apples, and an ancient sack of horehound candy to sweeten the stuff. Pouring it all together created a viciously aromatic swill that was the unfortunate color of snot.

Poor Wraque was still recuperating with ringing ears and pink skin from his near-death experience and was yet addled enough from the explosion he agreed to lend me his mule to pull my creaking wagon on my sales foray. Loading up my bottles, and kissing Phaegin goodbye, I went to make, if not a fortune, at least enough to presume my ability to make more.

The two major flaws to my plan were a dearth of population in the great Dakota Territory and a dearth of a population that had any two pennies to rub together. Stopping at well-distant houses to further distant houses I was turned away time and time again, hours and sometimes days between rejections.

Inside these houses I caught pretty glimmers and olfactory delights of Holiday cheer that even the most impoverished seemed to have engineered: fragrant evergreen boughs, spicy gingerbread, flickering candles and ribbon. Apparently I cut the figure of a complete ne'er do well with my snot-colored hooch and my crumpled unwashed garb, as I was not once invited inside one of those homey abodes.

In a week of wandering in dismal cold, and spending the nights bellied up to Wraque's mule, I sold only two bottles. Then, when I was mired in hopelessness, I stopped at a saloon in Deadwood and was granted a Christmas miracle.

Some fella had hit it big in a gold mine over by Sturgis, and he was celebrating his riches by buying everyone in the bar a drink who was willing to make a toast to his success. Toasting had been going on all day and the town had celebrated their way through every barrel of whiskey, every bottle of rhubarb wine, and every cask of sloe gin to be had in 20 miles. The now-dry bar was turning the celebration testy and my 67 bottles of elixirs were welcome as wings in heaven. I sold 63 bottles for a dollar each.

I stopped at the Deadwood General Store and bought a five-dollar ring for ten dollars, a loaf of bread to stave off hunger, a small bag of oats for the mule, and two peppermint sticks that I wrapped with a length of fine silk ribbon looped through the gold ring. I delighted in the image of presenting such a festive proposal for Phaegin's Christmas, imagining how happy she would be with me, how beautiful with the ribbon in her hair, how heartfelt her acceptance.

Then, as the shopkeep gave me directions back to Fiji and the assurance I could be there in a few short hours if I kept a steady pace, I further delighted in how warm that closet of mine was going to be, and how absent the smell of a mule.

I could blame the shopkeep's instruction, but it was more likely my lack of a sense of direction that brought me, eight long hours later, wandering lost in the dark hours. I was trying to stomach the idea of yet another night of unrelenting cold balancing teeth, stench, and fatigue, when I saw a glow of yellow ahead, shivering in the night like a dropped star.

I headed toward the beckoning glow with the fervor of one of the wise men and soon found the shimmering was the steady light through a window, cut by wind-tossed branches. Soon enough I found myself outside a roughsawn cabin. The building didn't look like much but smoke was redolent, and I sniffed the woodsy, homey scent like I could fill my belly with the thickness of the air. Inside, I imagined, all the delights of Christmas from plum pudding to pork pie awaited. I tied Wraque's mule to a tree, tried to slick my hair and coat into some semblance of respectability, and raised my fist to knock on the heavy pine door.

The man who opened the door of the little shack was built powerfully as a sledgehammer and had a mop of dark curls as wild and luxuriant as deep summer ivy. The pelt seemed so eager to grow that it was not content to remain rooted on the man's head but continued swirling down the side of his face and along the curves under his chin and nose and, I would conjecture, further down his neck, along his rotund belly, onward to his toes. He, although looking a bear, stepped backward at the sight of me and with a quick step and a graceful flourish ushered me in.

Entering the homestead, I was disappointed that my imagination had so let me down. Inside, though warm, there was not a sign of Christmas to be seen. In fact the place looked practically derelict with the glow of light emanating weakly from the wood stove and a flicker from a single kerosene lantern. There was not a ribbon, a package, a candy cane, or a candle to be seen. Indeed, the place was almost bereft of furniture. There was a rough cot with waxed ropes woven across the surface, a four-spindled desk on which a mound of pebbles were stacked, a trunk that had seen far too many years, a bag which certainly wouldn't do for Santa (its weft and weave in certain compromise), what looked like some sort of musical case leaned into a dark corner, and a ladderback chair that an old woman was sitting on. Two children, a boy and a girl looking to be maybe about nine, looked up wide-eyed from a palette by her feet.

When the bear announced, "We have a visitor!", the old woman and children all clapped as though I were on the stage.

I made the visitor's dance of stomping and hello-ing, rubbing my arms in show of appreciation of the warmth, then introduced myself.

"Edward Turrentine Bayard, pleased to meet you." I bowed and a giggle emanated from one of the children, I couldn't say which, and I heard the whisper, "Turpentine."

The bear shook my hand and said, "I am Roman." He gestured toward the old woman, "This is my mother, Deka."

The old lady grinned at me with not a tooth in her head, coal-black eyes, and her face creased into such a myriad of wrinkles it was hard to believe she was actually made of flesh and not carved of weathered wood. She spoke with an accent that buttered her words exotic as they rolled from her lips. She said, "Pleased to meet you, Edward Turrentine Bayard. I foresaw your arrival."

I didn't know what to say about that and so merely asked her to call me Ned.

Roman ushered his children into standing. The boy, who looked much like a miniature version of his father with a curly mop and sturdy build, was Lugar. He lacked any of his father's animation, however, and stood looking around the room as if he wondered which corner he was being introduced to. His hands shifted and turned lightly at his side as I told him it was a pleasure.

The girl was as far apart from her brother as could be. Where he was dark, she was so white as to almost be aglow in the dim room, with platinum hair and pale eyes. Whereas Lugar stood stolidly ensconced in whatever land his own thoughts took him to, she was as alight to circumstances as if she herself was in charge of making it all happen. She took me in with the sharpest of glances, seeming as though she had already sized me up and now knew my birthplace, pants size, and the fact that I was fearful of heights. She made a swooping curtsy, her bright full skirt swirling with a twist of her wrist. "Charmed."

It was a curious group to have sprung up here on the prairie. It was as though I'd found a ring of scarlet lilies sprouting through the snow and I wondered where they had come from. It seemed a forward question and so, as I accepted a seat by the fire, I instead asked Roman what he did.

"I am a farmer."

He looked no more like a farmer than I did. Further, when I had shaken his hand, I'd noted his palm was soft as risen dough.

Roman sat beside me and leaned on one knee, his tone changed from energized cheer to one of terrible gloom. He intoned, "I came to the Dakotas a young man but will leave it old indeed. This wretched land has aged me five fold in but a few years. When rain is needed, there is none. When sun is needed, there is rain. What will grow is eaten by locusts, the soil is blown away by the unending wind."

Deka, Sinta, and even Lugar burst into another round of applause. I was more than confused. "You are a farmer…"

Roman bellowed laughter. "Of course not, man!" He handed me a sheet of paper. It was a letter, yellowed with time. On it was penned the exact words that Roman had intoned. Under them was one more line. "I leave this piece of rock dusted with barren soil to whomever is foolish enough to want it. Sincerely, Lars Oppenheim."

Roman flicked the paper. "It was here with the deed on the table—and just like that, I am a landowner."

"Are you a farmer?"

"Of course not. I am a thespian! And what are you, Ned?"

The four of them stared at me, perhaps expecting a performance to match Roman's. I shrugged. "Not much of anything, really." I reached over and shook my valise. "I am a seller of cordials and apertif right now." I pulled out a sample bottle. "Made from the finest ingredients to be had, it will increase your appetite, ease your liver, and cheer your heart, all for only a dollar a bottle."

I recognized I had made an error in mentioning the price. Though dressed in colorful garb they were obviously rubbed raw by need: the weft showed in their clothing, Deka's toes poked from her the ends of her shoes, Sinta's hair looked like it had been chewed by weasels and overall they had such a sense of hunger and desperation I could feel a dull menace rise from the group. I amended my spiel. "But on Christmas Eve, they are nothing but gifts."

I presented Roman and Deka each with a bottle that they took as though I'd handed them each a gold bar. Roman surveyed his bottle and apparently saw no disconnect between my appearance and his subsequent conjecture: "You must make quite a profit with such a product."

I grimaced. "Likely the profit the product is due, unfortunately." I made ready to go, feeling strangely eager to leave the warm room. "Can you tell me which direction Fiji lies?"

Roman protested. "You aren't leaving are you?" At my ascertaining that yes I must go, he insisted, "You must drink with us!"

Sinta and Lugar leapt up, gathered around my waist, squeezing like a skirt two sizes too tight and demanding, "Stay! It's Christmas! Yes, yes!"

I insisted they let me loose, the effect of Lugar's grip in particular making me lightheaded from lack of oxygen, and I was almost certain one of them was trying to filch my pocket watch, but the children only released me when Deka shouted, "Vermin!"

Roman cocked his elbow and let fly. There was an abbreviated squeak.

The children clapped and shrieked, "You got it, you got it!"

I realized Roman had taken up one of the pebbles on the desk and flung it with such invective and sharp aim he'd gollywobbled an unfortunate mouse who now lay inert on the dusty floor.

Roman gave me a meaningful look, and I wondered if I was confederate with the mouse in some like jeopardy. Roman tossed a pebble from one doughy but alarmingly deadly hand into the air, catching it with a snap, and spoke with what

I discerned was an edge to his voice. "Let us hear a toast from our new friend, Ned!"

I wasted no time in taking a bottle for myself from my valise. We all jimmied the corks out with a resonant pop and made our toasts. I spoke most hopefully, "Here's to Christmas – Peace to all."

Roman raised his bottle to the webby ceiling, "Christmas— merriness to all!"

Deka raised hers and said, "Christmas—may we all be rich."

It seemed an extraordinarily hopeful toast on her part.

Sinta reached for her father's bottle and asked if she could have a drink. Roman shook his head, the curls swayed like kelp in a turgid sea. "I'm sorry my sweet, this is no Christmas for littles."

Sinta's light clouded a moment then she rallied and said, "Santa Claus will bring us our gifts in the morning." She addressed me: "Lugar has asked for a carved horse and Santa Claus will bring me a china doll with a lace dress."

Roman said, "Of course he will!"

I doubted this was so and thought it might be a bit irresponsible for Roman to agree so easily. I could not help but imagine the children in the morning, searching for their doll and horse or even potato gun and posy to no effect. I then thought of the peppermint sticks I'd purchased for Phaegin. She'd be just as happy with one of the sugary sticks as two, I figured, and so I disentwined the ribbon, ring and peppermint, slipping the ring into my pocket. I brought forward one piece of the candy, and snapping it neatly in half, handed a piece to each of the children, meriting heartwarming and gleeful thanks.

After another bracing drink of elderberry cordial I asked, "And what, may I ask, are you, a thespian, doing here?"

Roman sighed. "It was ardor that ruined me, for I am a man of animal magnetism."

I guffawed, thinking that this was yet another performance, much like his pretending to be the tired Swede farmer Lars Oppenheim. But Roman was not joking. He patiently continued. "You may doubt it, but I have the most beautiful woman in the world for a wife." He gestured toward his children. "Of course, you need only look at them to see what she must have brought to our union."

Lugar was back to vacantly staring at the fire, tapping his thighs methodically. Sinta smiled at me with sharp teeth, as if to dare me to say anything.

Roman continued, "I draw women to me, through no fault of my own." A pause. "It has happened before, it will happen again," he added sadly, as though Roman were anticipating bloodletting or perhaps an attack of gout. He went on: "Lugar, Sinta, Deka and I were touring with a masterful troupe—twenty-four of the most accomplished actors this side of the Platte River—to perform Shakespeare's Midsummer. Unfortunately, the wife of the director formed a desire for me and as a result the director kicked us out, right here, pushed me from my own caravan, sent my children after me and my mother as well, deep in the middle of nothing." Roman was as incredulous as if the director had ostracized him for breathing.

I thought about the situation. "But where is your beautiful wife?"

"She is home, waiting for me. Oh, she will be furious when she finds out what the director has done. In any case I expect she will come to fetch us soon."

I thought perhaps that it was true his wife would not be happy but wasn't sure it was going to be the director she was furious with, considering something more substantial than desire seemed almost certain to have taken place no matter Roman's protestations.

I nodded. "I also have someone waiting for me. My sweetheart, Phaegin." I stood and again said I must go.

Roman said, of course. He understood, and gave me brief directions to Fiji.

I tipped my hat and made my goodbyes, then departed into the frigid night, now devoid of stars. I wondered if it was going to snow, and wished I could see the moon for some point to reference direction.

I hoped if I gave the mule reign he would find our way home. I went to the lee side of the house but neither the mule nor the wagon were there. I circumlocuted the house, looking one way and another, praying, calling "Mule! Mule!" as if the animal had ever or would ever come when called. The damned creature likely did head home without me and I swore I would cause misery to the beast next I saw him.

The chill from the air give way to a heated desperation. I ran around the building again, still disbelieving my failure to sight the wagon. After the third time around I burst back into the house. "My mule and wagon, they're gone!"

Roman stood up and shouted, "No!"

"Yes!" I returned.

Roman went out with me to ascertain that there really wasn't a mule where I had left one.

"What could have happened?"

Roman wrapped his arms around himself. "It must have been wolves. The winter has been harsh and they are desperate and clever creatures, luring an animal into the darkness for their ravening dinner."

I eyed the man; he seemed truly horrified and the emotion was catching. Roman put his arm around me and led me back into the house. "The scourge of the county. Killed a man's oxen last week, one snatched a baby from a sunporch mid June.

Though I cautioned myself not to panic, it was too much not to. Not only had I lost the mule that Wraque would certainly over-bill me for and the money I'd earned on the cordials that had been hidden under the buckboard seat, but in doing so I had lost my right to ask Phaegin to be my wife. I slumped onto the creaking cot and stuttered, "Oh my Lord."

Roman slapped me on the shoulder and guffawed. "Of course the wolves didn't get your mule, Ned! There are no wolves in South Dakota. You have to go to the far reaches of Canada for that. Or maybe even Russia. I put your mule in the barn."

Sinta grinned with her pointy teeth while Roman soothed me. "The poor animal needed some oats and a rest. What kind of host would I be if I hadn't settled your mule for you?"

"Did you?" I wondered when he had accomplished such a thing.

"There are no wolves?"

"Not a one, a few bears perhaps. Further, I wouldn't actually be able to tell you how to get back to Fiji. I could better direct you to Minsk as this country is alien as the moon to me. It is a far more sensible idea for you to stay here with us tonight."

I felt somewhat weak with the pendulum of emotions I was experiencing threatening to bowl me over.

Roman patted me on the back. "Sit down, Ned, you look like you've seen a ghost." He chuckled, "You are the most credulous man I've ever met." He turned to his family and said, "It's our turn to give our new friend Ned a Christmas gift. Don't you think?

Deka said it was a fine idea as Sinta twirled and agreed. Lugar nodded.

I made one more attempt at escape, standing from my seat. But Roman pushed me back down insisting "Tut, you won't insult us for a half hour, would you? You've given us a gift, Ned, and now you must allow us to give one to you."

Deka shouted, "Vermin!"

Roman swiped another pebble, releasing it in one inexorable movement. There was a thud and squeak, almost simultaneous, and another mouse met its end.

Deka drew out a knife and stabbed it into the writing surface of the desk, causing the pebbles to rattle.

It seemed I should stay.

I finished my bottle and gave a dispirited smile. "What gift am I to expect?"

Roman wagged a fat finger. "It's a surprise. What would Christmas be without a surprise?"

"Just another day, I guess," I said weakly, wishing for just that.

Deka motioned me over to her. She picked up the knife and carved a shape into the surface of the desk that looked something like an egg with spines. She directed me to place my hand over the egg. My palm landed on the egg, each finger dropped on a spine. What luck, I thought, for her have to fashioned the symbol to fit my hand so perfectly.

Deka, with no warning, repeatedly stabbed the desktop between my fingers with such rapidity it was as if she were chopping onions. Indeed, it made my eyes water. Then it was over and when she told me to remove my hand from the table, I was almost unable to do so.

Deka peered at the marks made by her knife on the wooden surface. "You have a fine future ahead of you, boy. Many good things."

I realized this was to be a fortune telling and, feeling it wasn't the sort of thing that merited knife play, replied curtly, "I must say I am relieved to be meeting them with all my digits."

Deka scratched at the marks she'd made with the knife, apparently reading the language therein. "It says you will find a loving wife, you will find a vast fortune. Yes…"

She stared into my future intently and I mumbled, "But will I get home?"

"Ask me a question worthy of my skills, Edward. Something of love."

So I asked her for the date of my future marriage, figuring one that was in the near future would almost certainly have to be to Phaegin.

Deka nodded sagely. "I must go into my trance to see the date." She closed her eyes and hummed. I waited. In a few minutes the hum shifted to snoring and Deka slumped gently to the desktop.

Roman smiled a tender smile. "My mother is old, but an exceptional soothsayer. No doubt she will tell you your wedding day when she wakes."

He turned and addressed his son. "Lugar, take the stage."

Lugar was sucking on his peppermint. I raised an eyebrow as I'd noted the children had finished their candies a good half hour ago. I glanced at Sinta and she too was enjoying more peppermint. I conjectured that she'd been in my valise and as if to corroborate, she gave another wicked smile. I grabbed at my pocket and was relieved to find Phaegin's ring still there and was glad that I'd left my cash fortune in the wagon rather than in my bag. I glared at the girl with no little ire, not caring that she was just a child; she had the heart of a thief.

Lugar stuck the rest of his candy into his teeth and crunched it loudly as he trudged to the kerosene lamp and carried it close to the wall. The boy stood there and flapped his hands. I was saddened for this poor child and tried to put on an air of interest in whatever clumsy performance he was trying to give. He waved, he flapped, he curled his hands one over the other in what could only be a macabre dance.

Then I caught sight, beyond his hands, at the shadows that Lugar cast with his oddly positioned hands on the far wall. I saw Lugar conjure a wolf there. It opened its jaws and howled a long silent howl. Somehow Lugar made the animal's ears tremble, the throat undulate. The wolf then bent its head, the tongue came out and lapped at an invisible body of water.

Lugar shifted, pulling his shirt hem over his left arm. The boy's round belly shone in the light, but when Lugar lifted his other arm up into a right angle, a swan swam languidly along the wall, a wing magically fanned the air.

A fish leapt out of the water shaking its fins, a cat with a snapping tail batted at the fish. Each turn of the shadow brought a more complex and impossible performance. When Lugar returned the kerosene lantern to the table I clapped and hooted, though Lugar seemed not at all aware of my appreciation, sitting back on the palette by the fire, his hands fluttering as if practicing a new shadow show.

Roman kissed the top of Lugar's head, murmuring to the boy, then turned and called Sinta to turn.

I was growing a dislike for the girl, and when she pulled two puppets from behind her back, my dislike grew another size. She'd taken the mice that had met their end by Roman's pebbles and dressed them up. It was an act that I found somewhat repugnant, not a fan of mice living or dead. But what made it worse was that I no longer had any question of if Sinta had been in my valise, for she had dressed the mice up in the silk ribbons I had purchased for Phaegin's Christmas. I almost demanded she return the pilfered ribbons, but the knife blade still glittered in the writing table, and I wasn't sure I wanted the ribbons back under the circumstances.

One of the mice wore its ribboning like a cumberbund; the other was festooned in bows and streamers so that it looked like the rodent was wearing a red ball gown. I noted with a sickening lurch that a golden band graced the creature's furry neck. Incredulous I hastily checked my pocket again and this time, sure as Sunday, Phaegin's ring was gone.

I stood and shouted, "That's my ring!"

Roman put his hand on my shoulder and pushed me back into sitting. "You will get it back, no mind."

I again narrowed my eyes at the girl, not swayed by the cleverness of the rodents' costuming.

Sinta, unfazed at my evil eye, sat behind the trunk and made the mice dance along the top surface. It was ridiculous, as could be expected. But then, though I fought recognizing it as such, it became overwhelmingly hilarious. Sinta twitched and turned the little mice, their black eyes still shiny and whiskers aquiver, into the most absurd postures. Bowing and curtseying, tripping over their own feet, Sinta returned the mice to life. The creatures stole kisses from each other, had a tiff and cried. The gowned mouse ran toward her mouse partner only to have him raise her above his head and give her a twirl as if they were Chinese gymnasts. The mice flicked their tails, wiggled their toes. It was an amazement.

By the time the Sinta was finished my sides ached from laughter and I'd decided such thievery was a very good use of the ribbons, if not the ring.

Sinta curtseyed, then gave me a peppermint-scented hug. "Merry Christmas, Turpentine."

I grinned, forgiving her everything. "Thank you, and a Merry Christmas to you, Sinta. Now, may I have the ring back?"

Sinta motioned that I should help myself, but as I approached the vermin I could see that some of the twitching and flicking was due not to Sinta's genius puppeteering, but to the mice's return to consciousness. As soon as I touched the gowned mouse she squeaked and jumped up on stiff legs Apparently panicking at finding herself mummied with ribbons and choked with a gold band the mouse dashed to the center of the room.

I shouted in a panic, seeing Phaegin's ring escaping, "The mouse—it's alive! Get it!"

As the mouse zigged and zagged, amazingly agile with a ring and a goodly length of ribbon impeding its motion, we all stumbled around like oafish giants trying to grab a will-o'-the-wisp. Even Deka woke up and gamely tried to aid in the capture, though I wasn't sure she knew of what. She was more of trial standing in the way of the mouse's capture, yelling, "Where? Where?" while the mouse utilized her skirts as cover. Finally, just as I almost had my hands on it, the mouse scurried under the wood stove, to the back wall and into a small black hole in the timber behind

I plunged my hand as far as I could reach into the hole, scraping the hell out of my knuckles, but to no good. The mouse was gone, the ring was gone. I slumped against the wall, my hopes broken. "It's over. I can't believe it, it's over."

Roman seemed not at all concerned for me or the ring but that the incident didn't impede his schedule of events. He merely announced, "There are more rings to be had. Now it is my turn to play."

What was I to do? I pulled my hand from the hole and brushed the cobwebs off my shirt. I sat down, unable to register the magnitude of what had just happened.

Roman had the instrument case that I had seen in the gloomy corner in his hand. From it he took a strange sort of guitar with a scooped shoulder and a D-shaped hole in the front that gave the impression of the guitar smiling. The brass strings shone yellow where the lantern light caught them.

Roman commenced playing the strange guitar, plucking the strings and crooning in a deep basso voice. The music was simple but chords in a minor key made the lyrics somehow deeply sad and I remembered Roman's morose insistence that he drew women to him. It had happened before and it would happen again.

> He whistled and he sang 'til the green woods rang
> And he won the heart of a lady.
> She left her father's castle gate
> Left her own true lover

She left her servants and her estates
To follow the gypsy rover.
Her father saddled his fastest steed
And roamed the valleys all over
He searched for his daughter at great speed
And the whistlin' gypsy rover.
He came at last to a mansion fine
Down by the river Clady
And there was music, and there was wine
For the gypsy and his lady.

Roman entered into an extended solo, his fingers flying along the frets as though they weren't making the music, but dancing to it. I can't say how, but for a time the languid song erased my despair. I closed my eyes to see the shadowed dioramas that Lugar drew on the wall, the leaping mice running into embrace, could hear Deka's solemn assurance that love was mine and could see Phaegin's blue eyes and red hair as clearly as if she stood before me, and all was well and warm.

Roman strummed one final chorus of notes and I woke from the dream. Sinta sat cross-legged with her eyes closing, going limp into sleep aside her brother. Deka snored softly at the table, and Roman looked about him blushed with well-being. He walked about the room making his family comfortable with quilts and kisses.

It was a beautiful sight and though I was yet within the dream of well-being Roman's music had conferred, I wondered what would happen to the family tomorrow and the day after if the beautiful wife was as much a story as the mule-eating wolves. I wondered what story would be concocted to cover the dearth of presents. I wondered what they would eat. They were an amazement of a family, and though I'd lost the ring, I had to admit I'd had an amazement of a Christmas Eve.

The bear like man and I sat together and gazed at the room. I was quickly falling to sleep myself, but managed to relay my thanks to Roman. "It has been a sort of magic."

Roman looked abashed and gratified.

156

"Tomorrow I will return to my Phaegin," I continued, "and I'd like you to come with me. You will share Christmas with us, and while I don't want to insult you, I'd like to give you, lend if you like, half the money I've got to share. It should cover food, a few nights shelter and even something from Santa for the children-"

Roman put out his hand to stop me. "You are a good man, but my wife will come. She'll come with bells and toys and good food and kisses. I have no doubt." He made show of dabbing his eyes, then clutching his heart with both hands. "It is an honor you would offer aid to me. Like a brother, never an insult."

I went to insist but again he stopped me. "Let us sleep. Tomorrow is the day of days. All will sort itself out then."

He fell to sleep before I did, leaving me in the cacophony of his snores to contemplate the evening and anticipate the morrow. But not for long. Soon, I followed him to dreams.

The next morning I woke to chill and the fire in the stove having died down to a few lackluster embers. It was barely dawn but already the family was up. I wondered where they could be so early, and it took me a while to come out of a series of happy dreams to my senses to think clearly.

And to realize that, of course, Roman was gone, as were Deka, Sinta, and Lugar. I trudged outside and across the wide expanse of frozen ground to the old barn. Yes, they had taken Wraque's mule, and my wagon with the money I'd earned from the cordials still in it.

I was broke, marooned, betrayed and humiliated.

Roman and his family, in their haste to abscond, had left bag and trunk. My first impulse was to go through them hoping to find some identification, an address of Roman's wife, some way or means to send the constabulary to return my goods and dignity to me. But there was nothing there but cheap costumes and dogeared playbooks.

Further, it was ridiculous to look for an address, to even imagine I could find Roman through his wife. The man didn't have a wife, much less a beautiful one. The only magnetism Roman had was drawing fools in to sucker.

It was a sad and long Christmas morning for me. I tortured myself repeatedly with the image of Phaegin's Christmas morning. Did she think I'd abandoned her? Did she care? Perhaps she was enjoying the day with Randall Allan. My mind's eye saw Phaegin tearing open package after package of Randall's sweets and pretties, the prettiest of all his golden ring.

Would she accept it?

Would she be so foolish as to turn the good life away a second time? How could I love her and hope she would do so and wait for me, a useless, gullible, rube?

As the sun climbed to its cold zenith I heard the jingle of harness approaching. I ran outside and waved my arms about in the manner of a castaway flagging a ship.

The wagon soon enough approached so that I could see particulars of the driver, a woman with platinum hair braided to her waist. Her lips were red, her eyes dark, and she carried herself like a queen.

I could hardly believe it. I stuttered hello, practically struck dumb. Could this be Roman's wife? If so, he'd certainly not been exaggerating the woman's beauty.

She alit from the wagon and asked simply, with a thick Russian accent, "Roman—where?"

I was afraid to tell her he had absconded with the wagon, not sure if she would blame the messenger, or indeed if she was as much of a rake as the rest of her family seemed to be. I merely shrugged my shoulders.

She took it in stride and seeming to accept that I had little more intellect than the horse who pulled her wagon, did not introduce herself or ask my name. Indeed, she said nothing more and went directly in went to wait for Roman's arrival.

I followed her through the door. She took a look around, noted the dying fire, grabbed the ladder backed chair that Deka had been sitting on the night before and broke it over the back of the trunk. She picked up the pieces and stoked the fire. That done she sat down and took out a comb, unbraided her hair, combed it and did it up again.

She stared at me a bit, but didn't ask who I was and further didn't seem to care much when I volunteered the information. I finally ventured that I wasn't sure that Roman was planning on coming back.

She pointed to her perfectly shaped ear. After a moment I understood that she meant for me to listen.

In the hushed quiet I finally discerned a note or two of music. Could it be a guitar? I rushed to the door and flung it open. Far on the horizon I could see a wagon, hear the wind staggered notes of a song.

In but a few minutes I could discern that it was my wagon, pulled by Wraque's mule. Roman driving. Roman, Deka, Sinta, Lugar, and good God, Phaegin were all there. They piled out of the wagon, Phaegin and I laughing and clasping hands Roman, his most beautiful wife in the world, Deka, Sinta and Lugar all shouting in Russian and hugging. We had the most tumultuous and wonderful of Christmas greetings.

Roman's wife—whose name, I learned, was Lyvia—had indeed brought gifts, to the delight of the children. Lugar looked as animated as I'd seen any young boy, riding his stick pony as though he were Kit Carson, only grudgingly giving Sinta a turn on it so she could introduce her new china doll to the pleasures of horsemanship.

Phaegin brought food and after I'd helped unload the wagon (finding every penny of the cordial money intact in the box under the seat) we forthwith sat down to grand repast.

After we ate, I asked Roman why, if he had only meant to pick up Phaegin, he had taken his entire family with him to Fiji.

"My friend, I would not expect a woman of your caliber to get in a wagon with a man like me. And I did not want her to fall in love with me before I got her to you. So my family came to help." I nodded, glad Phaegin hadn't decided to throw me over for the hirsute man "Besides," Roman said, "What is Christmas without a surprise?"

Roman and I took a moment together to give one more goodbye. I gave him the last cordial I had left and a deerskin porch with twenty-eight silver dollars inside. He handed me a rolled piece of paper, a braided ring of platinum hair holding it closed. As Roman opened the pouch he exclaimed he couldn't possibly accept the money (even as he slipped it into his pocket) and I slid the ring off the paper and saw the document inside was the deed to the little house and ten acres on either side.

"Roman! You are giving me this place?"

He shrugged, "What is a house to an artist but a yoke on a blue-bird? It is yours, Ned. Don't let it age you overmuch."

He took me into a bearhug that was twice as uncomfortable as the squeezing that Lugar and Sinta had subjected me to. He climbed into the wagon with his family and they waved until they were small on the horizon.

Phaegin and I returned to the tiny house. I was feeling the warm success of Christmas, but when Phaegin pulled a package about the size of a man's fist from her pocket and gave it to me I realized I still had no gift to offer her. I slowly pulled the wrapping open and found she'd made me a cravat from patchwork pieces of silk she'd somehow located in the silkworm-less wilds of the Dakotas. I wrapped it around my neck and told her it was both beautiful and warm, just like her.

She stared at me expectantly.

I felt a little too warm as I thought of telling her how the sticks of peppermint and the ribbon met their end, hoping the story might be enough of a gift. I wondered if she would even believe the ring I'd meant to place on her finger was now circling a mouse's throat and wondered if I could blame her for not.

Burrowing my hands into my pockets I felt the cleverly braided platinum ring, slick and soft against my fingers. I pulled it out. It shone in the white winter light. Phaegin smiled, and I took my knee and pledged my love, a foretold fortune, and slipped the shining loop on Phaegin's hand.

ABOUT THE AUTHOR

Spring Warren is a Northern California writer. Read more about Ned and his adventures in *Turpentine* (Grove Atlantic) and about gardening in *The Quarter Acre Farm* (Seal Press).

THE MERRIEST OF MURDERS

KRIS CALVIN

The December Sacramento sky was a steely, starless grey, dark clouds coming in from the east, a threat of rain. It was only 7pm, but winter sunsets came early to California's capital. The thickly landscaped terrace at the far edge of the estate was dimly lit, so Johnny Jameson didn't see her until she stepped out of the shadows.

"Why are you in blue and silver?" the woman asked. "There's nothing jolly about blue and silver."

Johnny was uncertain how to respond—the large handgun she was pointing at him seemed to have short-circuited critical pathways to his brain. But he realized he had to say something.

If only to buy time.

Moments earlier, Johnny's mood had been light. Although his position as Chief of California's Health-for-All division was a powerful one, he'd once dreamed of being an actor. He'd arrived early at tonight's gala fundraiser to change into costume, and been directed to the secluded guesthouse since his grand entrance wasn't scheduled for another hour—it was to be a surprise to all but the Senator and, of course, the Governor who, per protocol, wasn't to be surprised by anything.

Now, face-to-face with a gun for the first time in his life, Johnny experienced an all-over numbness, a weakness in his muscles and joints. It took great effort for him to draw sufficient air to project his voice above the recycled water that flowed heavily from rock formations onto the surface of the nearby spa, which in turn fed the Olympic-size pool on the level below.

"It's to go with the theme," he managed to say. "Of the party. Winter Wonderland." As Johnny spoke, he forced his eyes from the weapon to two large french doors that led to the main room of Senator Stanton's modern and imposing three-story home, all concrete and glass. It seemed a great distance away, past the large spa, the pool and a garden of succulents rising up out of colored gravel, having replaced an expanse of lawn in deference to the ongoing California drought.

There were a few guests mingling about inside among uniformed catering staff, but hopelessness washed over Johnny as he realized no-one could see him or the gun–wielding woman in darkness at the back of the property. And although he had his phone, there was no way he could extract it from his pocket without her noticing.

The guesthouse was a simple, grey concrete building, but inside it was home to meticulously maintained mid-century furnishings, crystal planters filled with orchids and ocean-themed art on the walls. When Johnny arrived a garment bag was laid out on the bed, a bottle of chilled Napa Valley Schramsberg champagne in a bucket and Belgian chocolates on the nightstand.

Nice touch, he'd thought, pouring a glass of champagne before unzipping the garment bag and putting on his costume. Getting the false beard right was the difficult part, it hooked awkwardly over his ears. A wide black belt with an oversized silver buckle and heavy black boots completed his transformation from state bureaucrat to holiday icon.

"But you are Santa?" the woman asked, her eyes narrowing to near-slits as she gripped the gun tightly. "You are meant to make children happy?"

He wanted desperately to answer her correctly, it seemed important under the circumstances. Johnny looked down, as though to confirm. Despite the velvet suit he wore being powder blue rather than red, his firm stomach—a product of countless crunches at the gym—was padded to jiggle, and together with the full white beard made his identity unmistakable.

"Yes." He felt raindrops as he spoke, his head bare. He noticed the forgotten stocking cap in his hand, trimmed with white faux fur. He put it on, his hands trembling. "I am Santa."

"Good." She smiled and lowered the gun.

Johnny took a deep breath. It had to be a prank, he realized, her weapon can't be real. It was the holidays after all, he was wearing a fake beard! Then he saw her smile vanish as she raised her arms, the gun held with both hands, steadying her aim.

His mouth dropped open.

The first shot clipped his right shoulder. The second missed, but not by much. With the last she found her mark, the center of his chest. Johnny staggered backwards, falling over the unguarded edge of the terrace to the level below, where the rushing waterfall forced his body to the bottom of the silent pool.

To stay home, while tempting, would be the coward's way out, and California state lobbyist Maren Kane was no coward. Neither was she a beauty, she knew that. But her thick mane of deep auburn hair and arched brows above turquoise-blue eyes put her on the right side of pretty. Although that didn't mean men were knocking down her door.

Maren had always been awkward at flirting, and a history of failed serial monogamy hadn't improved her skills. Still, the holidays were no time to be alone in Sacramento—the legislature was in recess and the halls of the Capitol deserted—so she'd resolved to put the ugly break-up with her ex behind her, get out there and meet someone new. And what better opportunity than Senator Stanton's much talked about holiday gala? Plus, Maren figured even if she didn't meet an eligible man at Stanton's party, it was still likely to be an interesting evening.

The most famous member of California's legislature, Senator Stanton had recently published a best-selling autobiography featuring her transition from Michael to Michelle, which made her the first transgender elected official in the country.

Stanton had won her North Hollywood Assembly seat six years prior as a man. But while campaigning for re-election, Stanton was arrested for shoplifting an expensive necklace from a downtown Sacramento jeweler. Although legislators running afoul of the law was not uncommon in California or elsewhere in the country, Senator Stanton was facing a formidable opponent, an heir to a popular restaurant chain who had buckets of money which he invested in negative ads highlighting Stanton's arrest.

But when Stanton announced she'd been under duress when she took the necklace because she was coming to terms with the personal and difficult decision to embrace her true gender identity, enough voters applauded her courage that she edged out a victory. Since then, Michelle Stanton had been elected to the California Senate, moving up through leadership to chair the powerful Senate Health Committee.

Maren took another look at the invitation—Senator Stanton's image front and center in a silver gown, her dark hair piled atop her head in a prom-type style. The invitation specified "White and Silver Cocktail Attire".

Not something Maren had on hand in her closet.

Fortunately, the white, strapless, knee-length dress Maren purchased for the occasion had a side-zipper or she'd never have gotten into it on her own. She took a turn around her living room in her new three-inch silver heels to be sure she could do so gracefully. The shoes had their intended effect. Her legs looked longer and her ass higher than in the low-heeled red western boots she wore daily in the Capitol. Representing a fledgling eco-friendly toy company on issues related to the health and safety of children, Maren's boots, mid-length skirts and unstructured, jewel-tone jackets suited her firm's image. But tonight she was aiming for something sexy. Maren wasn't asking for much from Santa this year, but she did want to be kissed by a man—deeply and seriously kissed—before the New Year rolled in. As a final touch she picked up her silver clutch, cinched the belt on a midnight-blue trench coat and raised her collar against the December chill and first drops of rain.

Senator Stanton's front door opened directly onto a spectacular cavernous space with a vaulted ceiling three stories above the ground floor, a massive skylight in the center. The light rain beginning to fall beat a soft rhythm as it struck the glass.

A dozen seating areas with varied versions of chrome and white leather chairs and chaises were sparsely occupied when Maren arrived a little after seven. Guests, seated and standing, balanced drinks and hors d'oeuvres on small plates. Jasmine and pine floral arrangements infused the room with a fresh, outdoorsy scent. Nearly everyone wore white or silver, in compliance with the invitation. A woman in a gown that looked to be made of white feathers executed a complex jazz riff on a grand piano in a far corner, with a trio on stand-up bass, saxophone and drums providing backup.

"May I take your coat?"

Maren would have missed the young man at the makeshift coat check station to her right if he hadn't spoken. She removed her trench coat in exchange for a ticket that she tucked into her clutch, then headed towards a chair out of the main traffic flow. She wanted to get her bearings. This was the part Maren hated most about going to a party unaccompanied, the first few minutes where there was no getting around the awkwardness of being alone.

Then she noticed two men across the room, deep in conversation. Both looked familiar to her. In their late forties or early fifties, in great shape, she might have assumed they worked security for the event, if not for the drink each man held.

One was very tall, maybe six foot five, with a strong, pale face and a boyish bowl-cut of light brown hair. He had oversized hands that he couldn't seem to keep still, gesturing expressively each time he spoke or laughed. The other was of average height, stockier, his skin a soft caramel tone, with dark eyes and a full head of black, straight hair, nearly to his shoulders. He wore an off-white sports coat over a dress shirt and slacks in shades of black that didn't quite match. He seemed serious, although smiled broadly once at something the first man said.

A young woman circulating with a tray of champagne flutes offered one to Maren, which she accepted with the intent of making it last since she would be driving home later.

As she took her first sip, it came to her—the taller one was Sarunas Marciulionis! From Lithuania, he was the first Soviet-born player to be offered a spot in professional basketball in the U.S. He'd been one of Maren's favorites on the Golden State Warriors when she was growing up. She and her dad watched games from tip-off to final buzzer, yelling at the TV in unison when the refs blew a call and sharing high fives when Marciulionas executed a perfect shot.

Maren felt a pang of nostalgia for the days when she believed a love of sports could hold a father and daughter together, despite wildly differing natures. But then Marciulionas left the Warriors, ultimately landing in Sacramento with the Kings until knee injuries forced him to leave the NBA the next year.

That was also the year Maren's mother died, her father left, and nothing was ever the same again.

But here he was, in the flesh over twenty years later, Sarunas "Rooney" Marciulionas, his blues eyes sparkling as they met hers across the room.

Next stop, mistletoe...

The room was filling with more white suits and silver dresses worn by politicians, community leaders and fat-cat donors from Senator Stanton's Hollywood district. Tickets for the event ranged from $50 to $5,000 each—a large contribution meant bigger font for the attendee's name in the program and greater likelihood of his or her photo and a mention in the post-event press.

Several guests swayed in place as the jazz quartet picked up the pace with a Latin number. Others embraced friends and colleagues in greeting. Maren found the holiday spirit contagious, and although it had been fleeting she felt as though Marciulionis had looked at her the way she needed a man to look at her, it was what she'd been missing since she and Garrick split. She finished the champagne she'd planned to make last for the evening and picked up a second glass.

Maren estimated there must be over 100 people in the room now, and could see no clear path from the middle where she stood to where

Marciulionas was seated. The quartet launched into a jazzy rendition of I Saw Mommy Kissing Santa Claus, the high ceiling amplifying the bass notes against a blend of cocktail chatter and high-pitched laughter.

Mumbling "excuse me" over and over, Maren tried to squeeze through the crowd without spilling her drink.

This is not fun, she thought.

But then she reminded herself that being home alone in her pajamas with a good book, her dog Camper at her feet, wouldn't be preferable. Because while one evening like that might be nice, it could lead to endless days and nights of loneliness if she didn't make an effort to have someone new in her life.

As Maren approached her destination she took a deep breath, put on a smile and was about to introduce herself when a statuesque blonde in a low-cut silver dress appeared, placed her hand on Marciulionas' arm and said something to him in what Maren assumed was Lithuanian. The woman's mouth was turned down, her brow furrowed. Definitely not a party face. Marciulionas said something to the other man, then he and the woman abruptly left.

The woman might be the retired basketball player's lover or his sister, it was unclear. But the point of it for Maren was that Marciulionas, god-like on the court when she was a child, was gone. And he hadn't so much as glanced in Maren's direction before leaving. She felt her self-esteem plummeting through the oak floor she stood on, then shooting beneath the estate's concrete foundation before coming to rest somewhere close to halfway to hell. She eyed her silver shoes, wondering if she clicked the heels three times and repeated "there's no place like home" whether she might wake up in her own bed.

Then Maren felt the gaze of the second man. His look wasn't flirtatious. He appeared to know he wasn't what she had come for. She smiled tentatively and gave a small shrug as if to say, it is what it is. He reached out his hand to shake hers, then noticed her near-empty glass.

"Could I get you a drink? I'm Alibi. It's nice to meet you."

With effort, she tried to stay present for this man who was willing to speak to her, the one who hadn't left with another woman. Then she became aware again of the partygoers on all sides. "Thank you, but I think getting to the bar would require hand-to-hand combat."

He laughed, it was a pleasant, low, rumbling sound.

"Don't I know you from somewhere?" she said, then blushed as she realized that was pick-up line number one, at least old school it was. She didn't know what people said to one another in these situations now.

"It's possible." Alibi said, but offered no insight into how they might have met.

"Do you work in the capitol? I'm a lobbyist, so I'm there most days."

"I'm sorry, it's so loud. Did you say you lobby?"

"Yes. "She took a step closer to him so that he could hear, then stepped back, suddenly self-conscious in her strapless dress.

He took a sip of his drink, which looked like ice water, although Maren supposed it could be eight ounces of vodka over ice. "I don't get to the capitol often. I spend most of my time in South Sacramento."

South Sac included the tougher parts of town. Maren noticed again the man's muscular build. Putting the two together she realized who he was. Alibi Morning Sun, Chief Homicide Detective for the Sacramento Police Department. Maren had read a profile on him in the Sunday paper a few months back that reported that Alibi's mother selected the name because her baby son's birth provided her husband with an alibi for a murder charge.

"Who did you say you lobby for?" Alibi asked.

"It's Ecobabe. We specialize in environmentally friendly toys and games. A portion of profits is used to promote laws to protect children's health and safety."

Alibi motioned that he still couldn't hear her well, then guided Maren with one hand lightly on her arm towards an open spot against the wall. The two of them just fit between two large ficus plants, decked out for the season with silver ornaments and tiny white lights.

They talked about the rain and whether it would last, why Maren hadn't become a practicing lawyer after law school, and finally music— Maren liked everything but classical, Alibi was a symphony man.

She wasn't sure what she'd expected a homicide chief to be like. Glum, grave, angry? Alibi Morning Sun seemed none of those. He also was available—or at least he lived alone, he'd made that clear. His look had grown on her. Thick, black, straight hair that hung to his shoulders, deep brown eyes, strength apparent in his hands and in the way he carried himself. When he asked for her number, she gladly complied.

Maren watched Alibi tapping away on his phone and assumed he was entering her number into his contacts when a minute later her phone pinged. An incoming text from an unknown number with a Sacramento area code.

Does this count as a first date?

She looked up to see him smiling, but his dark eyes were serious.

"Well? Does it count?" he asked.

Unfortunately, rather than feeling happy that she'd found what she'd hoped for this evening—the possibility of romance—Alibi's use of the word "date" in his message seemed to set off some kind of warning system for Maren.

She remembered the trajectory of her two-year relationship with Garrick. It seemed to her that it started in a similar fashion. Fun. Respectful. Then morphed into white-hot passion before collapsing under the weight of Garrick's cheating and cruelty.

In fact, it struck Maren that her judgment had been so poor with respect to Garrick that she couldn't possibly trust how she felt about Alibi in such a short time now. Then her stomach rumbled. She'd noticed several buffet stations when she came in, heavy with silver trays. She wasn't sure she could eat anything without splitting the seams on her tightly fitted dress, but she was willing to try. And she reasoned that leaving the secluded spot might slow down the blind chemistry that seemed to be drawing her and Alibi inexorably together. If nothing else, food would buffer the effects of the champagne she'd drunk so quickly, and she could see if he still appeared attractive to her then.

"Are you hungry?" she asked him.

"Ravenous." She felt his eyes move from her face to her breasts, then to the hem of her dress against her thighs, giving his answer a second meaning.

She couldn't help it, she didn't mind.

They had taken only a few steps into the crowd when Alibi stopped and again pulled his phone from his pocket. He listened, said a few words, then gave Maren an apologetic look as he headed back to their spot by the wall where he could hear the caller. She mimed the act of using a fork and pointed towards the opposite side of the room, indicating she would hunt and gather for both of them.

But Maren discovered that securing food was not an easily attainable goal. Although she hadn't yet seen Senator Stanton, a majority of the other 119 California legislators and an equal number of their staff seemed to be at the party. Plus, there were lobbyists. So many lobbyists…every few steps Maren was waylaid by a colleague with a cheery greeting or a tale of woe about a sponsored bill that didn't get out of committee.

The event increasingly felt more like work than play. Maren decided to delay her mission to locate food and see if she could find a bathroom. Two glasses of champagne on top of two cups of tea before leaving home were taking their toll.

She was navigating with some difficulty through the crowd when she nearly knocked over Beth Connors, an elementary school teacher in her mid- twenties with whom Maren had worked on education bills in the Capitol, becoming friends in the process.

Beth's thin form seemed to have been swallowed up by an oversized red and green Christmas-themed sweater and a voluminous sparkly red skirt. She had either missed or ignored the evening's dress code. Beth teetered on red high heels—Maren could see she wasn't the only one who would have benefited from training wheels to manage her evening footwear.

Maren reached out a hand to steady Beth and found her sweater damp to the touch, she was shivering. "Are you ok? It must be raining hard now. Did you just get here?"

Beth glanced over her shoulder. When she turned back her eyes were soft with tears, her mouth tight. "I shouldn't have come…I…"

Beth's painful expression transported Maren back to an overcast day in Sacramento the December before, when she and Beth stood graveside as a small, white casket containing Beth's daughter was lowered into the ground.

Beth left last fall to earn a masters in education in Texas. But with the tree trimmed and the stockings hung in her small Houston apartment, two-year-old Carissa was struck by a high fever. The toddler suffered two weeks of unrelenting illness before succumbing to complications of the flu. Not ebola, not meningitis—garden-variety flu. An act of God, the Texas pastor had said.

Afterwards Beth went home to Sacramento, but took a leave from teaching. She couldn't bear being around children. She found a sales job at Macy's and spent much of her free time on Facebook, rearranging and reposting photos of the day Carissa was born, of Carissa's first steps, of Carissa holding her favorite toy. Each image held the promise of a future that never happened.

"Why don't we sit?" Maren asked, still an arm on Beth as she scanned the room for an empty couch or chairs. Beth broke free, openly sobbing, as she pushed her way towards the front entrance. Maren tried to follow, but the gaps Beth made through the groups of revelers closed quickly in her wake. When Maren lost sight of her altogether she texted her—there was no point in trying to speak on the phone over the holiday banter and music.

I'll meet you out front

A moment later, Maren's phone vibrated.

No, don't. I'm ok. I'm going home.

Maren didn't want Beth leaving alone when she was so upset, but she knew her friend would be gone before she could get to her.

Let's talk tomorrow. No response.

Maren felt warm, and with both hands lifted her hair off the back of her neck. The beginnings of a headache crept across her temples. A bathroom break had even greater appeal now, she wanted to splash cool water on her face.

A hallway to the left seemed a good place to start. En route, Maren passed large glass French doors leading to the darkened back of the estate. Rainfall obscured the view of what she imagined must be palatial grounds to match the scope and opulence of the Senator's home. At the end of the hall, a closed door bore a tasteful sign: "Powder Room". She was about to try the handle when she heard first a woman's voice, then a man's, followed by sounds of passion that in her experience more commonly emanated from a bedroom than a bathroom.

The hallway branched off to the right where she could see what appeared to be a small library or den. She figured she could wait there. Maren wanted distance from the lovers' soundtrack and to find a place to sit down before her three-inch heels hobbled her for life.

It was a comforting space. Floor-to-ceiling mahogany shelves packed with books of all genres, plush armchairs alongside polished wood tables, several with Tiffany reading lamps—the modern aesthetic of the main house abandoned for an escape into dark tones and lush textures. A sliding glass door looked out onto a gated courtyard, thick with colorful native flowers and plants.

Muffled music and laughter emanated from the main room, but the sound of rain in the background seemed to have stopped. Maren walked to the sliding door to get a better look and to her surprise found it open, nearly an inch. Sliding it the rest of the way, she stepped outside. A sliver of moon peeked from behind still-thick clouds. She could smell lavender and mint in the clean night air.

Maren wasn't sure of the appropriate amount of time to give the couple to consummate, but she thought 15 minutes seemed fair. It wasn't like they could settle in for the night—someone else in search of a bathroom was bound to stumble upon them, sooner or later.

A tall wooden gate at the back of the courtyard was ajar. Maren was curious what the rest of the property looked like. When she pushed against it the top of the gate scraped against branches of an acacia tree, causing heavy clusters of yellow flowers to shake and in the process giving Maren a good soaking, she let out a yelp. Then she looked down and saw that the form-fitting fabric of her dress was now sufficiently transparent to give her decent odds in a wet T-shirt contest. She wondered how long it would take to dry, and how she might get her coat back for cover without parading her new look—which had gone from sexy to slutty—in front of other guests. She decided to go around the side of the house so she could come back in the front entrance, within a few feet of the coat check. She forced the gate the rest of the way open and stepped through.

A moment later, modesty and fashion choices were the farthest things from Maren's mind. There was a horrific scream, a siren wail of terror unlike anything she'd ever heard as Senator Michelle Stanton staggered out of a gravel-lined bed of tall plants 20 feet from where Maren stood. The senator was barefoot, her floor-length gown torn at the bottom, her dark hair matted against her head, mascara running down both cheeks. She stopped screaming, but her eyes grew wide as she pointed at Maren.

"You...how could you?" the Senator shrieked. "You killed Santa!"

It seemed early to Maren for the party to have gotten this out of hand. True, Senator Stanton might have started drinking in the afternoon, although Maren was pretty sure seeing dead Santas was more likely to have resulted from hallucinogenic use. But since Stanton had come out as transgender, every aspect of her behavior was under a microscope and there was never any suggestion of drugs.

Maren took a few steps towards Stanton, hoping to calm the senator somehow, when what she saw through a gap in the tall plants stopped her in her tracks.

A man's body lay half in and half out of the swimming pool. On his back, his lower torso was in shallow water on the pool's steps, his head and shoulders resting on the concrete deck. The light blue costume he wore was stained on the front with what appeared to be blood. He stared, unblinking, at the night sky. Maren had no doubt that he was dead.

Her heart was racing, she felt dangerously close to passing out. She took a deep breath, then exhaled slowly. But she knew no amount of measured breathing was going to calm the panic overtaking her. Because as soon as she had glimpsed the man's face she knew she might as well find Detective Alibi Morning Sun, hold out her wrists and let him cuff her. The man lying there, the one evidently intended to cheer partygoers with his imitation of a blue-suited Santa, was Johnny Jameson, head of the government's Health-for-All initiative. A man who only a week ago 30 people had witnessed Maren threaten to kill.

A young, uniformed police officer stood at attention just inside the door to the library, staring at a spot well above Maren's head. It appeared that making eye contact with her was not sanctioned in whatever rulebook he was following.

Maren felt sick to her stomach. She was seated in one of the large chairs, hugging herself, covering her chest. She asked to use the bathroom, having failed to accomplish that earlier. Her voice sounded small and far away to her. The cop removed a walkie-talkie from his belt and within minutes a woman officer arrived.

Maren's first attempt to get out of the chair was unsuccessful. Her legs trembled, then threatened to buckle underneath her.

It felt strange to be standing outside the small bathroom again, although this time the door was open, the couple long gone. The officer waited in the hallway while Maren executed the difficult task of inching her damp, tight dress up and her panties down in order to pee. As she washed and dried her trembling hands she dropped the small bar of soap, then the hand towel. Control of her motor skills seemed to have been impaired by the double blows of seeing a dead man and being accused of his murder.

Maren's escort dropped her back at the library. The young male cop was gone, Alibi Morning Sun paced the room. "Sit," he told her, motioning to an armchair. His mouth was grim, his voice flat. He took the chair across from her.

Maren felt tears starting at the corner of her eyes. She wiped them away as quickly as she could. Whatever had passed between them earlier that night, it was clear she wasn't going to be able to collapse into Alibi Morning Sun's arms for comfort.

He started speaking as soon as she sat down. "This estate is fully fenced, front to back, with a modern security system, including cameras and alarms."

That made sense to Maren. Senator Stanton's celebrity status undoubtedly made privacy difficult to obtain. She also remembered reading that the Senator received threats after coming out as transgender.

"We haven't found any breach of the system," Alibi said, "so it seems unlikely that someone got to Mr. Jameson from outside. Not impossible, but it means we're focusing our investigation on people permitted access to the estate during the time in question—guests and staff." Although Alibi didn't say it, Maren knew she had a special status on that list since Senator Stanton had publicly accused her of the crime.

Alibi tapped his phone to open a note-taking app, then asked Maren to describe her actions since arriving at the party, being as specific as she could.

Maren prepared carefully for testimony in the capitol. She knew from experience that when she didn't she had a tendency to go off on tangents. But since the "prove you didn't kill someone" presentation she was about to give hadn't been booked in advance, she fell back on what she learned in law school as advice to witnesses of any kind.

Stick to the facts.

"I arrived alone. I had a glass, no, it was two glasses of champagne. We met. You and I…" She hesitated, then decided additional description of her interaction with Alibi wasn't needed. "I left to find dinner, but couldn't make it through the crowd to the buffet. I looked for a bathroom…"

Her sentence tailed off, incomplete, as she experienced a full-body chill and a bout of dizziness. She closed her eyes to keep the room from spinning and involuntarily pictured Alibi removing his jacket, wrapping it around her, telling her she would be okay.

"What happened next?" he said.

When she opened her eyes, Alibi's expression appeared unfeeling, his mouth a straight line. Removing his jacket to comfort her seemed the last thing on his mind.

Maren felt anger taking precedence over her feelings of physical shock and sickness.

If Alibi Morning Sun wasn't going to see that she was taken care of, she would damn well do it herself. She'd done nothing wrong and she was determined she would not be treated like a criminal any longer.

"I'm very cold," she said. "Do you think you could get me a blanket or coat or something?" Although posed as a request, Maren spoke loudly and clearly. There was no doubt she was making a demand.

Alibi frowned, then stood and opened the door to the hallway. He exchanged words with someone before returning to his seat. "Officer Lee will find you a blanket."

"Am I under arrest?" she asked firmly. "Should I have a lawyer present?"

He seemed to consider his words carefully. "No. Senator Stanton's reaction when she saw you raises questions, ones for which I will need answers. But you don't have to speak to me without a lawyer if you prefer to wait."

She wasn't sure what to do—she had minimal experience with criminal matters, her focus was the "legalese" used to write laws. Since she hadn't killed anyone, she figured one approach would be to answer Alibi's questions honestly. But, there was also the possibility that her answers wouldn't clear her of the crime, in which case she should not offer more information without an attorney.

Maren was given a reprieve in her deliberations when Officer Lee appeared, carrying neatly folded velour sweatpants, gold with red trim, and a matching zip-front hoodie, both emblazoned with the University of Southern California fighting Trojans logo. Maren returned to the bathroom. The dry clothing seemed to make everything better, despite her being a CAL Berkeley grad who wouldn't normally be caught dead in USC colors.

Back in the library, she found her hands steady as she accepted a protein bar and water bottle from Alibi. She didn't know if it was wishful thinking, but his eyes seemed softer, even kind. In that moment, Maren decided to answer his questions without waiting for a lawyer. It wasn't just that he seemed less hostile, although that was part of it. It was also that now warm and dry, her head relatively clear, it had occurred to Maren that this interview wasn't only about determining her guilt or innocence, or at least it didn't have to be. Information she provided might help the police to locate the real killer.

"When we took a break, we were at the point where you said you'd just used the bathroom," Alibi said, consulting his notes.

"No. It was occupied."

"How did you know? Was the door locked?"

"I heard voices, male and female…sounds." She felt herself blushing. Even in this context, she didn't want to have this conversation with this man. "My best guess is they were having sex."

Alibi raised an eyebrow, but made no comment.

"I came here to wait. I walked to that glass door, over there." She pointed to the slider. "It was open. I went outside to get some air."

"Open? It was unlocked?"

"It was unlocked, but it was also actually open. An inch or so."

Alibi nodded.

"I wanted to see what the rest of the estate looked like." She reached her hands up and rubbed the back of her neck, fighting a wave of fatigue. "A drooping branch of a tree got bumped when I pushed the gate. The flowers on it were heavy with rain so I ended up getting soaked. I wanted my coat…"

"Why did you want your coat when your clothes were already wet?"

"My dress was white, so getting wet meant …" Maren could feel her cheeks coloring as she held her hands open in front of her chest to indicate the problem.

Alibi looked away, down at his phone. But not before she caught the hint of a smile on his face. When he looked up his tone was definitely gentler, more conversational.

She had known men who couldn't accept that they might not be able to protect a woman from pain or sadness. The stereotype was the man who couldn't stand when a woman started to cry, and would withdraw coldly or might yell at her to stop, even if he cared for her. She knew it was a stretch to assume that kind of emotion might overtake a cop during a murder investigation, but she considered it a possibility. Because now that she seemed stronger, less in need of him, Alibi was behaving more like the man she'd met at the party. The one who asked whether their conversation counted as a date.

"I thought it best to go around the side of the house, and then back in the front where the coat check was set up. That way the fewest people would see my…" She realized that sentence needed no end, and went on. "But I didn't have a chance, as soon as I was out of the courtyard Senator Stanton was there."

Maren took a breath, remembering how awful those next few minutes had been.

"She pointed at me and said I killed Santa. She looked disheveled, her hair, her make-up. I thought maybe she was drunk. But then I saw Johnny, I mean I saw his body. By the pool. I don't remember what happened exactly, but pretty soon there were a lot of people outside, I guess they'd heard the senator scream. One of her staff brought me here."

Alibi's eyes rested a moment on hers, he seemed to be searching for something there. "Just a few more questions. Then we can find a room where you'll be able to lie down. We're not detaining you. But if you stay it might save us from having to bring you to the station for further questioning in the morning." He scrolled through his notes before speaking again.

"Did you know Mr. Jameson, the deceased?

Maren marshaled what little energy she had. She sat up straight. Whether Alibi was leaning towards believing in her innocence or not, she knew that what she said next mattered.

"I was appointed to a community-based task force to advise Johnny Jameson and his staff at Health-for-All. We focused on strategies to ensure that every child in California would have access to a medical home—a doctor to see regularly. None of us knew Jameson, he'd come here from a private sector position, I think it was in Florida or Texas."

"What was he like?" Alibi asked.

"Smart, high-energy. But it was hard to tell whether he was personally committed to the mission of health care for children." Maren's throat felt dry. She picked up her water bottle and took a drink.

"Last week Senator Hindall announced that he planned to introduce a bill to close nonprofit clinics in California and shift that funding to a for-profit organization. He argued it would serve patients more efficiently and save the state money." She took another sip, then set the water down. "But Hindall and his staff hadn't done their homework. The major for-profit company in that market, LILHealth, was under investigation in five states for deaths, including two children. Critics say LILHealth has failed to deliver adequate preventive care— regular physicals, hearing and vision screens, vaccines."

"I'm not sure I follow," Alibi said. "How does Hindall's bill involve Jameson and you?"

Maren nodded, she was getting there. "Someone leaked emails showing that Jameson is the one who sold Hindall on the idea to move funding to LILHealth. Being new, Johnny might have felt pressure to show that his division could provide care at a lower cost—nothing illegal in that. But then a reporter found that Johnny was on LILHealth's payroll before he came here, and rumors flew that he would get kickbacks from his old employer if he was able to open the door to the lucrative California market."

There was a knock at the library door. It was Officer Lee. Alibi stood, the two men turned their backs on Maren and spoke in near-whispers. "I've got to go," Alibi said, grabbing his sports coat. "I'm sorry, Maren, we'll finish later."

He was part way out the door, but Maren wasn't done. She wanted to go home. She wanted something better than a protein bar to eat. So she stood and continued. "I told Johnny Jameson that he should be the first to sign up for LILHealth services in California, because if anyone was going to die from their shoddy, substandard care, it should be him." She swallowed hard. "I shouldn't have said it. But I did, and it got tweeted out, going viral. It was everywhere: Ecobabe Lobbyist says Jameson should die first."

Alibi's phone buzzed. He told the person to hold and turned back to Maren. "Wait for me, can you do that? Officer Lee will be in the hallway if you need anything." He didn't stay for her answer.

As soon as she was alone, Maren let out something close to a growl of frustration. Shouldn't Alibi have asked her a few questions before he ran out? Like did you want Johnny Jameson dead? Or better yet, did you kill Johnny Jameson? Wasn't this the moment when she got to explain Senator Stanton's mistake and proclaim her own innocence?

What could possibly be more important?

Then it hit her. If Officer Lee told Alibi that they had discovered evidence pointing to someone else, that they were on the track of the real killer, then Maren would no longer be a suspect. It was the only thing that made sense to her. She'd been holding herself together through sheer willpower since Jameson's body was found. The kernel of hope she was allowing herself to feel now, that this craziness might be over, was enough that she stopped fighting her fatigue and curled up in one of the oversize chairs, soon drifting into a welcome, if unsettled sleep.

<<>>

The back of Senator Stanton's property was lit up like a nighttime movie set, a half dozen stationery lights set at intervals, black electrical cords snaking through thick foliage to outlets and generators. The rain had stopped, but blue tarps elevated on stakes were strategically placed to protect the equipment in case the bad weather returned. Alibi, in dress shoes, made his way carefully across the still-slick slate patio to the far edge where his team stood at a makeshift command station.

Rachel Codghill, junior detective in homicide, was in charge of the crime scene. Her short, bleached blonde hair with black roots made her look more like a punk rocker then a cop. Next to her stood a young, ginger-haired and freckle-faced officer, Clyde Watson.

"Evening, sir," Detective Codghill said. "I can give you a rundown on what we've found at the scene. Then Clyde—Officer Watson— will update you on the status of interviews with guests and staff. Unless you'd like the other way round."

There was a loud crash as someone tripped on one of the cords and knocked a light over on the upper terrace. Alibi turned, saw it was being handled and returned his focus to Rachel. "What do we have in terms of physical evidence? Since his jacket was soaked in blood, it's a good guess our guy didn't drown. But I'm assuming you'd have told tell me if you found the weapon?

"38 revolver, standard."

Alibi raised his eyebrows. "We have it?

"No." Codghill stuffed her hands into her pockets and stamped her feet. The temperature was in the high 40s. "But we have a bullet. The killer missed once and we got lucky, it was close enough to the guesthouse that we picked it up on the first search."

Alibi nodded. They'd caught a break there, it would take time before the coroner dug any other bullets out of the victim.

"Also, we found footprints on the second level. The hour of rain didn't have much punch to it, plus thick cover from tree branches up there sheltered the ground. One set is clearly the victim's—they match running shoes found with his clothes in the guesthouse. Then there are the boots Jameson had on. Prints show he walked from the guest-house towards the edge of the terrace, stood in one spot for at least several minutes, causing deeper indentations." Rachel demonstrated Jameson's actions as she spoke, taking a few steps, then standing still. "He backed up, looks like he was staggering, the weight distribution between his feet was uneven, before falling over the edge."

"Any chance he was pushed?" Alibi asked.

"Looks like he fell from the way the footprints skid."

"So, putting the location of the bullet and the trajectory of his footprints together, Jameson was shot there," Alibi said, pointing to the second terrace "...and fell into the pool, below. But how did a dead man get to the pool stairs, half out of the water?"

"Senator Stanton said she found Jameson's body floating face down and dragged him over to the stairs to see if she could save him. That fits with her shoes being off and her dress and hair drenched."

"But that doesn't rule out Michelle Stanton having fired the shots herself, then afterwards coming down to the pool and pulling Jameson out. To make it look like a rescue." He looked up towards the feature-less concrete guesthouse, picturing Stanton firing her weapon, then coming down the rock-hewn staircase to the pool, moving Jameson and screaming for help. "She wouldn't be the first killer to feign dis-covering the body," Alibi said.

A cold wind came up. Codghill moved to her left, hoping for bet-ter shelter at that angle. "There were also a woman's footprints on the top terrace. Barefoot. Senator Stanton was shoeless when she accused Maren Kane of the murder." Codghill was shaking her head as she said it. "But the footprints on the top terrace are a woman's size seven. The senator wears a size 11. A man's size 11."

Alibi looked down to give himself a moment. When he first met Maren Kane that evening he'd found her more interesting and attrac-tive to him than any woman in a long time. The next thing he knew she was a suspect in a murder that he was investigating. Then he'd allowed himself to become convinced that she didn't do it, that her supposed threat against Johnny Jameson was nothing more than political posturing in the capitol. Now it was clear from the evidence that the killer was a woman, person unknown.

He tried to picture Maren's feet. He'd noticed her silver high heels, it was hard to miss them at the end of those long legs. But were her feet big, small, or average? And for that matter, was a size seven women's shoe big, small or average?

He texted Officer Lee and directed him to ask Ms. Kane if she would mind sharing her shoe size. He figured if she tried to make a run for it rather than answer, at least they'd have gotten somewhere. He turned his attention to Clyde Watson.

"A member of the Senator's staff, Ginger Lassen, reported greeting the victim at the front door to the Senator's home at 6:45 PM. Ms. Lassen was instructed by the Senator to provide Mr. Jameson with any support needed in his role this evening." Clyde took a breath. "Lassen walked Mr. Jameson to the back door and indicated the location of the guesthouse on the second terrace, where his costume was laid out for him. She offered to walk him up there, but he declined. Lassen obtained Mr. Jameson's cell number and told him she would text when it was time for him to come down, when all the guests, and in particular, the governor had arrived."

"The Governor?" Alibi asked. He'd forgotten that Governor Caries was supposed to be in attendance. "Did he…?"

Rachel Codghill cut in. "Governor Caries was running late. We were able to reach his team when Jameson's body was discovered and divert him from coming."

Alibi let out a breath. At least that was one problem he didn't have to deal with. He signaled to Clyde to continue.

"Ms. Lassen texted Mr. Jameson at 7:45 to let him know the governor was delayed and that Jameson's entrance as Santa would be pushed-back. Jameson didn't respond. Lassen told Senator Stanton, who said she'd check on Jameson herself. It was 15 minutes after that when the senator announced she'd discovered the body."

"So that puts the time of the murder at between 6:50 pm, when Johnny Jameson left to go up to the guesthouse, and 8:00 pm when

Senator Stanton says she found the body? That's scarcely over an hour. While the coroner may be able to tell us something more, I doubt we'll narrow the window. Speaking of which, where is Sandy?" Alibi could see from where he stood that the body had been moved from the edge of the pool, so the coroner's initial assessment must have been done.

"Sandy's lying down. In the guest house," Rachel said. "He's not feeling well. He said to let you know you could speak to him there when you're ready." Codghill was clearly trying to suppress a smile. It was common knowledge that Sandy Zane, the coroner, was always sick with something. Alibi would get to Sandy when he finished with Clyde.

"And where are we with the guest interviews?

"Done."

Alibi was sure he'd heard him wrong. "You've interviewed over 100 guests?"

"Yes, sir. 134. I have an app for it, sir. I modified one that companies use for hiring. It permits me to rapidly scan IDs, so I have name, address, birthdate, all that, in a few seconds." Clyde paused, he appeared uncertain how much detail to give. "I altered the fields to address questions about each guest's whereabouts during the party, including if they had witnesses that could place them inside the house during the time in question, and whether they saw anyone leaving who they knew, so that we can identify people we need to talk to who might have left."

Alibi was stunned. "Did you create this application this evening?

"I've been working on it for awhile. This is my first use of it in the field, though, and I didn't anticipate trying it out with so many people." Watson adjusted his glasses, shifting from one foot to the other, apparently nervous about what his boss's reaction would be to his innovation.

"Terrific, Clyde." Alibi said. "Anyone you think we should look at?"

Clyde considered the question. "With the party occurring in one big room, since it was raining and all, everyone had a similar story. They arrived through the front entrance sometime after seven and stayed inside all night. Neither the kitchen nor the bathrooms directly off the main room provided access to the back yard." He scrolled and clicked a few times. "But there are two people, Tina and Tim Simpson, who said there was a line for the main bathroom so they went and found another. Sounds like they were gone for 20 minutes or so from the main room. I didn't have them point out the location yet, but I can talk to them. I guess especially her, given the footprints.

The Simpsons' story matched what Maren had told him. Alibi was surprised to hear the couple was married to one another, though. Seems they couldn't wait until they got home. Good for them, he thought. He turned to go up and look at the scene by the guesthouse.

"Sir, one more thing," Clyde said. "Several guests mentioned seeing a women head down a hallway off the main room. I checked it out, there's access to the back of the estate from there. No-one saw her return." Clyde scrolled through his notes. "The woman's name is Karen…no, sorry—autotype." Clyde tapped the screen. "Maren…it's Maren Kane."

Alibi checked his phone, nothing from Lee yet. He was tempted to go back to the library and find out her shoe size himself. It wasn't so much that he was hearing anything conclusive that pointed to Maren. It was more that there didn't seem to be anyone else who looked good for Jameson's murder. He wondered how long it would be before he would have to read Maren Kane her rights…

His thoughts were interrupted when Rachel Codghill spoke up. "I have a call from the coroner. He'd like you to come to the guesthouse now. He says it's important."

When Maren awakened, she had a stiff neck from sleeping in the chair. She felt far from refreshed. Alibi hadn't come back, and had failed to deliver on his promise of a room where she could lie down. She knew she was cranky, but really, he was rapidly proving himself to be useless. She opened another protein bar and tried to make sense of what she knew so far.

The senator's holiday party was supposed to have been her chance to breakout, to have some fun. Instead, Maren had found herself a suspect in a violent murder. And on a lesser, but still disturbing note, she'd had to share one of the lowest moments of her professional life with a man she thought she might be falling for.

Maren knew her behavior at the last task force meeting had been inexcusable. While politicians often get away with public displays of anger, it can cost lobbyists their jobs. Maren felt fortunate that the consequences for her had been limited to a stern reprimand from the Ecobabe Board, as well as the clear message that she should not expect a holiday bonus.

The only person who seemed to understand and even support Maren's outburst was Beth Connors. Beth had told Maren she agreed that Jameson needed to be stopped and that Maren was a hero for publicly saying so. Maren was surprised at Beth's passion, since Beth had stayed on the sidelines of political advocacy after Carissa's death. But then Beth shared that it was LILHealth's Texas division that wouldn't pay for Carissa to be seen by a doctor until it was too late. Maren was glad to see Beth funneling her grief into something positive— testimony from Beth when the Hindall bill was heard in committee might be just the thing to cause the legislature to be thoughtful regarding the LILHealth funding decision.

Maren wished there was something she could do for Beth. She remembered her sobbing as she left the party, and realized the one-year anniversary of Carissa's death had hit her hard—Maren couldn't imagine what it would be like to lose a child. Maybe they could go out for an evening after this was over, when the real murderer had been caught and Maren was off the suspect list.

But then, as the phrase "real murderer" floated around in Maren's mind, something else struck her about her memory of Beth tonight. When she almost knocked her over, Beth's sweater was wet as though she'd just been out in the rain and she was shivering from the cold. At the time, Maren assumed Beth had just arrived at the event. But as she replayed back the interaction in her mind, she realized Beth hadn't been coming in from the front entrance, but rather was walking in the opposite direction, through the crowd from the back of the estate.

Beth was coming from the place where Johnny's body was found. Maren stood up, her dizziness returned. She felt a sharp stab of pain in her stomach. She realized she might throw up. She leaned heavily on a chair as she considered the conclusion she had just reached, that it was Beth Connors who killed Johnny Jameson.

<<>>

"I understand he wanted me to wait, but I need to speak with Alibi, now!" Maren felt at a disadvantage trying to pull rank over a uniformed police officer when she was wearing a gold and red-striped jogging suit, but she was not taking no for an answer.

"I've texted him, he's not picking up. I can't let you disrupt a police investigation…"

Maren leaned right, then dodged left, employing a basketball move she'd used in college when guarded by much taller girls, then took off at a dead run past Lee. She skidded as she made the turn at the powder room out to the now empty main room. Her intent was to exit the french doors to the back of the property and find Alibi herself, but the door was chained with a padlock, evidently to prevent contamination of the crime scene. She changed course and headed back the way she'd come, slowing to a dignified pace when she was in sight of the library.

Officer Lee was still there. Not only hadn't he chased her, he hadn't left his post. He said something into his walkie-talkie, she assumed calling off whatever pursuit he'd put in motion, and stepped aside to let her back into the library.

Maren was happy that Lee seemed to believe that she had learned her lesson when confronted by the locked exit—that the back yard was absolutely off limits—and that she would behave herself and wait patiently for Alibi.

Not even close, as she planned to keep on walking through the library and right out the courtyard sliding door.

But once she got inside the room she saw it was time for Plan B, as there was a new officer, one she hadn't seen before, sitting outside in a chair by the gate in the courtyard.

For someone who wasn't being detained, Maren was definitely feeling a "you're a detainee" vibe.

She found her silver clutch, sat down facing away from the courtyard, pulled out her cell phone and texted Alibi.

Connors is killer.

Then she realized he might not know what that meant.

School teacher Beth Connors killed Jameson.

Call off the hounds. I'll explain.

It was then that she noticed there was a Plan C. In front of her, partially hidden by heavy silk drapes, was a large double-hung window. She had closed the door on Officer Lee (she didn't slam it, as none of this was his fault), and the cop in the courtyard couldn't see her from where he sat.

She eased over to the window. It didn't open easily, she needed to use both arms and put her weight into it. She wasn't sure whether the side yard opened onto the back of the estate, but at a minimum she could yell over the fence and have somebody get Alibi's attention. She put one leg over the window sill, then the other and was on her feet on the gravel pathway just in time to see Beth Connors coming from the front of the estate, still in her party clothes, a large red purse clutched in both hands.

Maren's hand flew to her mouth. She couldn't imagine what Beth was doing back at Senator Stanton's, and she wasn't sure she wanted to find out.

When Beth saw Maren, she smiled fleetingly, but her face was drawn. As she got within a few feet she moved back against the hedges along the fence. When she spoke it was almost a whisper. "I have to talk to you."

Maren said the first thing that came into her mind. "How did you get inside the estate?"

Beth toyed with a strap on her purse. "When the driver of an SUV stopped to talk to the cop at the gate, he was distracted, it was easy for me to pass by the other side. They're watching for someone trying to get away, not for someone trying to get back in. "Beth paused.

"I know you've been arrested. I saw it on Facebook. I'm here to help you."

Arrested?

Seeing Beth in her poufy skirt and holiday sweater, stating that she was here to help, Maren had a moment of doubt. She found it hard to hang on to her earlier conviction that Beth Connors had killed Jameson. Perhaps Beth was coming from the back bathroom when Maren ran into her earlier, or had been out getting a breath of air in the courtyard. Things Maren had done that made her a suspect. Beth certainly looked anything but dangerous right now. Maren stepped closer to her. "I haven't been arrested."

Beth shook her head. "There are photos of you on the internet with the senator, she's pointing at you. The arrest is public. Is the Governor ok?"

"The Governor?"

"He was shot. Not with Jameson. Later."

"Beth, that's not true. Someone from the event must have posted a photo of the senator and me and then it became an old-fashioned game of telephone. Each person who posted got the story a little more wrong, until it was all wrong."

Beth shook her head again, her eyes tearing up.

Maren's brow creased in sympathy, she spoke softly. "I know you're upset, and with the anniversary of Carissa's passing…"

"It was Tuesday, one year ago, almost Christmas." Beth's tears started again, rolling down both cheeks as she reached into her purse and withdrew a gun.

The blood drained from Maren's face.

But Beth didn't point the weapon at Maren. She was examining it, turning it over in both hands. Then she looked up, her eyes glassy. "I had to. You know I had to. You're the one who made me realize it had to be done." She cradled the revolver, holding it tightly against her chest and rocking back and forth. "You were right. What happened to Carissa can't happen to anyone else." She rocked faster, shifting from one foot to the other as though she were comforting a fussy baby, rather than a 38 revolver. "When Carissa took sick they wouldn't give me an appointment, some advice person on their phone line told me to give her Tylenol, that fevers are normal in young children." She looked down at the gun, seemed to realize suddenly that she was not holding a baby. "You said if LILHealth came to California that more children would die. You said Johnny Jameson should pay!" She gestured wildly, the gun still in her hand.

Maren ducked.

Beth saw Maren's response and dropped her arms to her sides. "I have money saved up. We can drive, maybe to Mexico. They shouldn't blame you, they shouldn't. But since it was your idea, the police won't let you go." She began walking towards the front of the house at a determined pace, until she looked back and saw that Maren wasn't coming. Beth kept her voice low, but her tone was urgent. "We need to leave now."

Alibi felt like as though he'd aged 10 years in one night as he started up the path to the guesthouse to meet the coroner. He told himself not to care, that what happened to Maren Kane was no longer his concern. They hadn't spent more than 20 minutes together, so what if it felt intimate? It must be the holidays, creating the illusion that wishes come true. He reached for his phone and realized he'd left it at the command station with Rachel. He'd pick it up on the way back.

He was halfway up the stairs when Sandy Jones emerged from the guesthouse. Pale, white-haired, stooped with thick glasses, he looked every bit like someone who spent most days in the morgue.

"Alibi, what on earth took you so long? I've got to get home. This virus will be the death of me if I can't get some sleep."

Sandy was always certain he was about to die of something. Alibi was surprised all coroners didn't feel the same way. Or maybe they did, but Sandy was the first he'd worked with who could compete in hypochondria at the championship level.

"I gather we know the cause of death, a 38, "Alibi said. "And time of death was between 6:45 and 8:05 PM tonight. Anything else I should know?"

Sandy coughed, then wiped his brow. "He was already dead when he hit the water. One bullet to the shoulder, inconsequential, but the second took out his heart." He coughed again.

Alibi turned his head away, hoping Sandy hadn't cried wolf so many times that Alibi was now in the presence of something actually contagious. "Thanks. I look forward to your report."

"Oh, I almost forgot. When I'm sick I don't think as clearly. I don't know if one of your officers shared this with you or if they thought I would. The deceased had his phone with him when he fell. Some kid is working to see what he can get from it."

Some kid? Alibi scanned the area and saw Clyde Watson bent over at one of the tables under the lights. His strides lengthened as he hurried over to him.

"It's a Sony Experia Z," Clyde said. "It's cool. Really cool. Waterproof." He had the back off the phone, the battery out. "But either due to the velocity of the fall or the pressure of the rushing waterfall, it definitely got wet where it shouldn't have. I've on with tech support." Clyde gestured to another phone on the table, in speakerphone mode. "I called Sony, they patched me through to AT&T's emergency line."

Alibi was beginning to realize this kid was a valuable asset.

"Can I help you?"

The voice was tinny. Clyde picked up his phone for a clearer connection.

"Uh-huh…Okay…Thank you. Yes, ma'am, that would be good. Thank you." Clyde looked at Alibi. "They ran a system trace. The last active signal from Jameson's phone was 7:18 pm, before the elements in the phone got wet, and shorted out. She's emailing me over the documentation.

"So that's when Jameson fell into the water? 7:18?"

"Yes sir."

"A minute or so after he was shot?"

"It seems so, yes sir."

Alibi stepped away, pulled out his own phone from his pocket and opened his texts.

Does this count as a first date? Time-stamped at 7:22pm. Maren Kane had been talking to him at 7:18pm, at the time of the murder.

Alibi realized he was Maren Kane's alibi…He thought he might actually have felt his heart lift. True, he no longer had a clue who the real murderer was. But it wasn't Maren. And that was a good thing.

Alibi started walking, then jogging towards the library to speak with her. When he arrived, Lee was saying something about a text, about not reaching him, something about Maren running. Alibi was only half-listening. He wanted to tell this woman—this beautiful, stubborn, a little bit crazy woman—right now, that she was in the clear. He wanted to tell her more than that. He ordered Lee to go see if Rachel Codghill needed help. When Officer Lee continued to object, Alibi made clear he was having none of it, and Lee complied.

But when he opened the door, Alibi was faced with a wide-open window and an empty room. He ran over and stuck his head out.

Maren was standing still, her back to him, while a woman in a strange, fluffy red skirt and a holiday sweater waved a 38 revolver in the air. Upon seeing Alibi, the woman steadied the gun with both hands and took aim. She looked like she'd had practice. Maren turned and saw who Beth was aiming at just as Alibi pulled out his service revolver, clasped it in both hands and aimed back.

Maren stepped between the two.

"Maren. Move!" Alibi yelled. He was constrained by the window frame. He couldn't get a clean shot around Maren. He couldn't risk firing.

Maren stayed between them.

Beth took two steps to the side, her intent clear. As she tensed to pull the trigger Maren bent low and threw herself forward, tackling Beth hard at the knees. Praying as she did so that she was out of the line of fire.

She was.

But Alibi was not.

<<>>

Maren shifted in her chair, setting down the magazine she'd been unable to read.

Alibi's hospital room was small but private, with a window overlooking F Street, where a gentle rain was falling for the second time in as many days. Sacramento holiday shoppers didn't seem bothered as they sheltered wrapped packages under recently-purchase umbrellas.

Maren wondered what it would be like to be out there now. Because inside, it seemed to her it would be hard for things to get much weirder.

She was engaged in a bedside vigil for a man she had just met.

A man she barely knew.

A man whose life she had saved.

The bullet sailed off target when Maren knocked Beth Connors down, causing it to graze Alibi's arm instead of hitting him in the face. Or the heart. Or somewhere else really bad.

He opened his eyes, blinked twice and closed them again.

Maren couldn't tell whether he'd seen her or not, until he spoke. His voice was dry and raspy, his eyes still closed.

"Does this count?"

He lay motionless. Maren thought he might have slipped from consciousness again.

"I said, does this count?"

Maren stood up, leaned in and pressed her lips to his, lightly. He opened his eyes and encircled her with his good arm, pulling her towards him, where he gave her a kiss.

A deep and serious kiss…

ABOUT THE AUTHOR

A former local elected official, Kris Calvin's debut political mystery novel *One Murder More: A Maren Kane Mystery* is published by Inkshares. Educated at Stanford and UC Berkeley in psychology and economics, Kris has been honored by the California State Assembly and the Governor's office for her leadership in advocacy on behalf of children. Kris is an avid Northern California sports fan (Warriors, Giants and Niners). Learn more about Kris at www.KrisCalvin.com.

www.ingramcontent.com/pod-product-compliance
Lightning Source LLC
Chambersburg PA
CBHW070849120626
46556CB00002B/934